Letters from Pemberley
The First Year

A continuation of
Jane Austen's
Pride and Prejudice

Jane Dawkins

D1022530

Chicken Soup Press, Inc.
Circleville, New York

Chicken Soup Press, Inc.
P.O. Box 164
Circleville, NY 10919

Library of Congress Cataloging-in-Publication Data

Dawkins, Jane, 1945-
Letters from Pemberley, the first year : a continuation of Pride and prejudice / Jane Dawkins.
p.   cm.
ISBN 1-893337-00-6 (pbk. : alk. paper)
I. Title.

PS3554.A9458L48   1999
813'.54--dc21   98-56074
                                                        CIP

Second Printing

Book and cover design by Netherfield Productions,
Pine Bush, NY
Text set in 12 pt. Bodoni Bk BT
Printed by Worzalla, Stevens Point, Wisconsin

10 9 8 7 6 5 4 3 2

Dedicated with humility
to the memory of
Jane Austen
in gratitude for countless hours
of reading pleasure

Letters from Pemberley
The First Year

Introduction

At the end of *Pride and Prejudice* Jane Austen thoughtfully tells us how the story continues. After all, one never wants a good book to end and yes, it *is* satisfying to know that Lady Catherine does eventually become reconciled with her nephew, that Kitty shows great improvement removed from her sister Lydia's influence, that Georgiana and Elizabeth become fast friends, and so on. Indeed, Jane Austen's letters show that she knew her characters intimately and exactly how their lives would continue after the books ended. In his *Memoir* her nephew, James Edward Austen-Leigh writes, 'She would, if asked, tell us many little particulars about the subsequent career of some of her people.'

Nevertheless, despite Miss Austen's thoughtfulness, we want more! It is a mark of her readers' affection for her books that so many sequels to them have been written. Here is another — well, not quite.

My own particular wondering has always been about Elizabeth's first days at Pemberley, her bewilderment perhaps, her anxieties — the every-day of a new life as wife and mistress of Pemberley. Although she is a gentleman's daughter (as she forcefully reminds Lady Catherine de Bourgh at the end of *Pride and Prejudice*), she suddenly finds herself in a very different league of wealth and privilege altogether, mistress of a large house, and surely aware that many will consider that Mr. Darcy has married beneath himself. Notwithstanding the support of a loving husband, she must sometimes have felt insecure and alone and rather isolated during those early days. It was this 'little bit (two Inches wide) of ivory... with a fine brush' aspect of Elizabeth's first *days* at Pemberley that I have attempted to explore, rather than the larger sweep of the *years* which follow the end of *Pride and Prejudice*.

I think, too, that Elizabeth would have sorely missed her favourite sister, Jane, with whom she had such an intimate relationship, and decided that since they would probably have written to each other often and frankly, this book would take the form of a series of letters to Jane, written over the course of that first year at Pemberley.

Rather than a 'sequel' then, this book more closely

resembles an old-fashioned patchwork quilt, where in place of the scraps of fabric reminding one of the favourite frocks or shirts whence they came, there is a line or a phrase or a sentence from one of Jane Austen's books or letters stitched alongside the lesser scraps of my own manufacture. (A sequel, I think, would be a brand-new frock altogether!) Lovers of Jane Austen will relish, as I do, her wonderfully concise, witty and waspish, delicious way with words, and will recognise some of them. (Lately I re-read a book by one of Jane Austen's 19th century heirs, or rather heiresses, and was caught by one sentence which I felt sure Mr. Darcy might have said, so have taken the liberty of including it in my patchwork, hoping Miss Austen might have agreed it was not inappropriate, and that some of my readers might have pleasure in finding it for themselves.)

Similarly, favourite characters of mine from her other books appear in this patchwork with different names, sometimes borrowed from another of her novels or a word-play on their original name, sometimes a name associated with Jane Austen's life. I hope the reader will enjoy identifying them.

Like others, my love of Jane Austen's books led me to an interest in her life and times. It is from this interest that real life persons such as Henry Raeburn and Humphry Repton appear in my patchwork, along with contemporary ideas on architecture and gardening and art. Mr. Darcy has always struck me as a forward-looking, modern man who, mindful of the responsibilities of his heritage would, I think, have been interested in new farming techniques to improve the land on his vast estates and would have wanted to leave his own mark on Pemberley for future generations.

As I have tinkered with my patchwork, rearranging, adding, subtracting, putting back again — all with the greatest of ease thanks to modern technology — I have thought often of Jane Austen with her pen and paper and wondered how *she* managed when she had a better thought and then a better one again. Knowing how arduous a task continual re-writing would be (and well aware of the cost of paper) perhaps she only put pen to paper after she had first honed her wonderful prose to perfection in her head. One day I hope to see some of her original manuscripts to get an inkling of how that brilliant mind worked.

Some readers may take issue with me for setting this book in the year 1813. My defence is that although Jane Austen wrote *Pride and Prejudice* in 1796 and 1797 (then titled *First Impressions* and probably in the form of an exchange of letters) she revised it extensively before it was finally published in 1813, so that in my mind *Pride and Prejudice* ends at the close of 1812.

And this is probably the place to say that although I have tried to be historically correct (or approximate), I am no expert on either the period or Miss Austen: this book's only purpose is to entertain. If the reader is as entertained in reading it as I have been in writing it, I shall be satisfied. The more I find out about Jane Austen, her works and the society in which she lived, the more I want to know; it is a never-ending fascination.

Jane Dawkins
Walker Valley, New York

Letters from
Mrs. Fitzwilliam Darcy
to
Mrs. Charles Bingley

3rd February 1813
to
8th December 1813

Letter No. 1

Pemberley
Wednesday, 3ᵈ February 1813

*M*y dear Jane,
    Can it really be only several *weeks* since our joyful nuptials and tearful farewells? There have been so many changes, so much that is new since then that it all seems a lifetime ago.

I write to you from the comfort of my sitting room, which formerly belonged to Lady Anne, Mr. Darcy's mother. A pretty room, not overly furnished, with a little writing desk which is very much to my liking. Mr. Darcy has instructed me to make whatever changes I want to this room and to my private apartment, insisting they should be exactly to my liking and taste. Perhaps when I truly feel that Pemberley is home I shall, but for the time being I am happy to leave things as they are in their faded, comfortable elegance. Nevertheless, the honour of my dear Husband's gesture in giving me this particular room for my own is not lost upon me, and already I spend a great deal of time here when Mr. Darcy has business to attend to. The pleasing view from the window is an added attraction, the more so since I understand it was one of Lady Anne's favourite prospects. Even at this time of year there is a stark kind of beauty to Pemberley's surroundings and yesterday's snowfall has given the austere winter landscape a magical aspect, which is all the more pleasing from where I sit in my comfortable room in the warmth of a good fire.

We agreed to spend the first weeks here quietly and alone so that I can become accustomed to my new life out of the glare of the notice of the neighbourhood, who are naturally anxious to inspect the new mistress of Pemberley. Although tact prevents him saying as much to me, Mr. Darcy cannot be unconscious of the fact that some of his acquaintance will consider that he has married beneath himself. Perhaps he feels that his wife will be better able to hold her own in the face of any resentment, real or imagined, once she feels settled at Pemberley and begins to think of it as her home. Had we been able to actually discuss the matter I would have agreed with him wholeheartedly and thanked him from the bottom of my heart for his generous consideration of my comfort, but it is yet too delicate a subject to embark upon.

Notwithstanding our mutual desire for this quiet time, Mr. Darcy felt an obligation to order the church bells to be rung and to arrange a wedding celebration for his servants and tenants. This took place a week ago. Jane, I had not an idea that so many people were under Mr. Darcy's protection, and was quite astonished at his knowing so many particulars about them all — the names of children, a wife's recovery from illness, the addition of a barn, the success or failure of a crop. My heart swelled with pride as I saw not only the ease with which he conversed with everyone and accepted their congratulations, but also the respect and admiration in which my dear Husband is held by one and all. I recollected my surprise when, on showing us Pemberley last August, the housekeeper had declared Mr. Darcy 'the best landlord and the best master that ever lived.' At the time I had thought this excessive commendation, but I begin to see that she spoke only the truth. (Your own sweet nature would not wish me to say so, yet I must acknowledge that you alone, dear Jane, will not share my astonishment: you, who from the very beginning of our acquaintance with Mr. Darcy defended his character.)

The servants' hall was decorated with evergreens and ribbons and looked very festive. Mr. Darcy had engaged musicians and he and I led the first dance to much applause, though we had the good sense to remove ourselves early that the revellers might better enjoy themselves unencumbered by our presence, and so the dancing continued until ten o'clock, followed by supper.

Georgiana will join us from London in ten days and it is agreed that together we will begin visiting and carrying out those necessary social duties which will probably give little pleasure to either of us. Mr. Darcy and Georgiana are both uneasy and shy in social situations outside the family, and their circle is therefore small, so at least I shall be spared the agony of close inspection by a multitude! But it will be a trial of sorts for all three of us: *Mr.* Darcy will be anxious for his acquaintance to approve of his wife, and for his wife's approval of his acquaintance; *Miss* Darcy will be anxious to please her Brother by pleasing me; *I*, of course, am anxious to please Mr. Darcy by pleasing his acquaintance! What a circle of anxiety, one which I will laugh myself out of sooner or later, I am sure, though I fear that it is too early to begin teasing my dear Husband and Sister out of their share.

Yet I shall not scruple to confess to you, my dearest Sister, that amid all this elegance, and notwithstanding the affectionate heart of my Husband and our real happiness in each other, there are days when I feel quite heartsick: for your company most of all, but also for Longbourn and our quiet, ordered family life — even Mamma's nerves provoke a certain nostalgia! The enormity of Pemberley, beautiful as it is, and the responsibilities of being its mistress sometimes threaten to overwhelm, but my courage, so far at least, has risen to the occasion. I flatter myself that nobody but myself, and now you, knows my worries and uncertainties, least of all my dear Husband, whom I would not wish to cause pain and who, as you see, does everything in his power to please me.

No, you will think me an ungrateful creature, so let me hasten to add that everyone here at Pemberley makes great efforts to make the newly-minted Mrs. Darcy (how strange that still sounds!) welcome, showing extraordinary kindness beyond that which duty would require. If they do have any doubt of my competence and fitness for the role of mistress of Pemberley, they are good enough to keep it to themselves.

The housekeeper, the very capable Mrs. Reynolds, has been kindness itself. (On my fateful first visit here with my Uncle and Aunt Gardiner last August, it was she who showed us the house, neither of us suspecting, of course, that we should meet again under very different circumstances less than twelve months later.) Mrs. Reynolds has been at Pemberley since Mr. Darcy was four years old and appears to have sincere affection, pride and respect for the family. Although she has carried out her duties more or less alone since the death of Lady Anne, she very tactfully seeks my advice and instructions on matters which we both know she is more than competent to handle herself. Indeed, if I hesitate in venturing an opinion she will diplomatically suggest the right thing to do, then thank me as if it had been my own original thought — a valuable ally and teacher, whose respect I hope to earn in time. It occurs to me just now that I must be making progress; lately I find myself looking forward to, rather than dreading my daily conferences with Mrs. Reynolds. In the bewildering first days here I fancied I should as soon prefer a daily audience with Lady Catherine de Bourgh than have the good Mrs. Reynolds witness any shortcomings I might reveal!

Far above all in these early, uncertain days at Pemberley, my dear Husband's affectionate heart and generous consideration of my feelings on entering his home have been a tower of strength. On the afternoon of our arrival, for instance, which happened to be a sunny, if cold day, Mr. Darcy, perhaps sensing my feelings of trepidation at that moment, suggested a walk and retraced our steps along the very same path by the river, up through the woods and back across the bridge that we had taken that August day with the Gardiners. The familiarity of the circuit and Mr. Darcy's kindness in suggesting it were a great comfort to me. His sensitivity to my feelings on becoming mistress of Pemberley is just another example of his affectionate heart, and might very well astonish some of our Longbourn and Meryton acquaintance, more used to an air of selfish indifference.

The estate takes much of his time (actually demanding more of it than he has lately been giving), but he sees that we spend as much time as possible together. We take ever greater pleasure in each other's company, deepening our understanding and affection for one another. Our walks around Pemberley are some of my most precious times, even if the weather is yet too cold to walk very far. Mr. Darcy has a deep attachment to the woods and grounds hereabouts and knows them well. He takes great delight in pointing out the spot where he once fell in the stream as a boy, or a favourite tree he and Wickham used to climb, or a good spot for nutting. During these rambles, our conversation often turns to the earliest days of our acquaintance and our first impressions of one another, and our amazement (still) and gratitude that things have turned out so happily. That such painful memories can now provoke smiles is a wonder, is it not?

When the weather does not permit a walk outdoors, we take one indoors, perhaps along the gallery, where I am becoming slowly acquainted with the all too many Darcys whose likenesses hang there. Or Mr. Darcy might take me to one or other of the many rooms at Pemberley to point out, relate the history, or recollect a fond memory of some object perhaps, or painting, or piece of furniture. By sharing his knowledge or pleasure in it, he seeks to impart its familiarity to me. I could not wish for a more attentive, loving Husband, whose dearest wish seems to be that his wife should grow to love Pemberley as much as he himself does.

And so, my dear Jane, please be assured that I am happy with my new life. Your generosity will, I hope, allow me the luxury of sharing with you my small anxieties and insecurities, knowing you will not give more weight to them than they deserve — we both know that I will be laughing at them (and myself) before long. Until then, it is a great relief and comfort to be able to write to you in the open, frank manner in which we have always communicated.

My only wish now is that you are enjoying equal happiness with your dear Bingley at Netherfield. Not so, I do have another wish — for a letter very soon from you, my dear Sister, filled with as much happiness as you like and news of our family and friends.

Yours very affectionately,
E. Darcy

Letter No. 2

*N*eed I say, my dearest Jane, how welcome your letter was to me? Thank you for the immense pleasure it brought. Selfishly, it had not occurred to me that you might have anxieties of your own settling into *your* new life and home. Forgive me, I thought only of myself so far away from you all and imagined you happily settled at Netherfield, within easy reach of our friends and acquaintance, everything familiar and nothing to cloud your daily joy. Had I been a more considerate Sister I might well have imagined the possibility of friends and acquaintance (and yes, even family) being within *too* easy a reach of Netherfield. But perhaps you are right, once the notion of Miss Jane Bennet as Mrs.

Charles Bingley and mistress of Netherfield is no longer the novelty it appears to be at present, you will be able to lead a life less encumbered by overly attentive neighbours. Your forthcoming stay in London is an excellent idea and will enable them all to become accustomed to it in your absence — and your sweet, patient nature, which would not wish to offend, and Mr. Bingley's easy temperament, are spared even *thinking* about otherwise remedying a tedious situation!

Will Miss Bingley be in town when you are there? I understand she was mortified by our marriage but we have received very civil messages from her via an acquaintance of Mr. Darcy's and she writes very affectionate letters to Georgiana. I hope you will find her company tolerable and that she will feel a sense of obligation to pay off every arrear of prior incivility to you as befits her Brother's wife.

Georgiana has arrived from London. Mrs. Annesley, her companion, accompanied her here but has now left us for several weeks to nurse an ailing sister. In her sweet, shy way Georgiana shows me real affection and I am confident that with time we shall become fast friends. Her disposition is cheerful and open, without conceit or affectation of any kind, though she is clearly astonished to hear my lively, sportive manner of talking to her Brother, and to see him as the object of open pleasantry. The walls of Pemberley, I fear, have been unaccustomed to the sound of laughter for too long and here, at least, I may be able to exchange my role of willing student for that of teacher.

Now that Georgiana is here, my dear Husband is free to devote more time to business matters which have been sadly neglected since our arrival here, a consequence of his solicitousness for my comfort. Very timely too, since otherwise I would probably be in great danger of becoming a shameless, spoiled creature, fit for nothing but constant adoration and effusive praise! As it is, since it is still too cold for much outdoor activity (though there are signs of Spring), Georgiana and I spend a good part of each day together, often in Georgiana's very pleasant sitting room, which was fitted up by her Brother just last summer after she had taken a liking to the room. It has a graceful elegance and lightness which befits its owner. You will be amused that the music room sees me more often now that Georgiana is here, and I may say that her example of constant practice has encouraged my own fingers to follow suit. I know you will find this news surprising, since I was never known for taking trouble to practise.

I am very happy indeed that Kitty is spending time with you at Netherfield. Although she is already eighteen I do not feel she is entirely beyond the reach of amendment and, removed as she now is from the influence of Lydia's poor example, I hope that she can be just as easily persuaded that vanity and idleness should not be the business of her life and will come to see the advantages of improving her ignorant, empty mind.

Papa intends to pay us a visit during the summer and writes that he dearly looks forward to seeing Mr. Darcy's library, which pleases Mr. Darcy enormously, the library being a source of great pride to him. Begun by his grandfather and nurtured by his Father, Mr. Darcy has taken up the reins of responsibility most enthusiastically and constantly seeks to improve and add to it. I think my Father will not be disappointed by what he finds, and dare to hope that this common interest will promote a closer understanding between him and Mr. Darcy.

You ask about Charlotte. Just after our arrival here she wrote that because Lady Catherine is still in high dudgeon about Mr. Darcy's marriage to me, she had wished to delay her return to Hunsford for as long as possible. Her condition, however, obliged her to make the journey much sooner than she would have wished. Poor Charlotte, as the dearest friend of the person who thwarted Lady Catherine's plans for an alliance between her daughter and Mr. Darcy, I am sure Lady Catherine's attaches some blame to her for the shades of Pemberley being polluted by me, and so Charlotte must suffer the consequences. While we were still at Longbourn I believe I told you that since Lady Catherine's offensive reply to Mr. Darcy's announcement of our betrothal, all intercourse between them is at an end, so any attempt by *us* to mollify her would merely fan the flames of her indignation. I have no doubt, however, that Charlotte's good sense will prevail, and surely Mr. Collins's extravagant daily civilities will help to smooth Lady Catherine's ruffled feathers in time?

Tomorrow we go to Hurstbourne Park, just five miles from here. In my honour, Sir Richard Mansfield, an old family friend of the Darcys, has kindly gathered together most of his, and consequently Mr. Darcy's, intimate circle to meet me formally. This is to be a much smaller affair than Sir Richard had in mind; his original plan, Mr. Darcy tells me, was for a grand ball to take place the week of our arrival. Mr. Darcy was adamant, however, that his wife should not be overwhelmed by visitors and social obligations immediately, and his acquaintance has respected those wishes, even though they may not fully comprehend them.

Apart from a few informal morning visits (at which I feel I passed myself off creditably) this will be my first real social outing of any import. So, your Sister is to be thrown into one large den of lions rather than several smaller ones and should be suitably grateful for it, I suppose. Let us hope that my stubbornness that never can bear to be frightened at the will of others will carry me through, since I am quite determined not to feel intimidated, and equally determined that my Husband and Sister will be proud of me.

And so, my dear Jane, you may imagine me in my suit of armour, spear in hand, setting forth to subdue the discontented horde; my head held high, a smile on my face, and always your devoted, loving Sister,

Elizabeth

Letter No. 3

Pemberley
Thursday, 4th March, 1813

*O*h, Jane, thank you for your confidence that all would be well and that the den of lions would turn out be no more than a basketful of adoring kittens. Not quite true — about the kittens anyway — but I am pleased to be able to tell you that all went very well at Sir Richard's, and I feel that there is great relief all round that everything passed off as well as it did. I will not pretend that there was no initial discomfort (and not just on my part). Indeed, so great was my agitation and so fearful was I of not doing exactly what was right, and of not being able to preserve their good opinion, that in the embarrassment of the first five minutes, I could almost have wished to return immediately to Pemberley — nay, to Longbourn. My courage prevailed, however, and by the time the evening came to an end and the carriages were called and we all said how much we were looking forward to meeting again, I believe most of us actually meant it. I shall not feel embarrassed about being in their company again, though I am not yet *quite* able to hope for it very soon.

You asked for all the particulars of the occasion and I shall attempt to leave nothing out. I wore the yellow sarcanet (made up in Meryton last November, you will recall, in the same style as your pale green muslin with the round neckline and darker green trim). After much deliberation I decided against wearing any of the Darcy family jewellery in favour of my own simple topaze cross. Mr. Darcy was a little disappointed until I explained that for this first formal occasion I should prefer to appear as my own unadorned self, without pretension, and not impose myself right away as the new, grand Mrs. Darcy, complete with Darcy finery. He understood my sentiments exactly, I am happy to say, and I believe my decision stood me in good stead, for Mr. Darcy told me afterwards that several people whose opinion he values, including Sir Richard himself, congratulated him on his wife, particularly pointing out their admiration of her simplicity and lack of pretension. As for admiration, it is always very welcome when it comes, but I do not depend on it; so do not be concerned that, following my small triumph, my bonnets are now several sizes too small.

Let me attempt to describe the group to you, beginning with our host, Sir Richard Mansfield, who is a well-looking man of about forty. His countenance is thoroughly good-humoured and his manners friendly. Renowned for his hospitality and generosity, he has lately been especially kind in assisting a widowed Cousin with two daughters (left in distressed circumstances, I understand) by giving her a cottage on his estate, and all transacted in such an easy manner that she and her daughters should feel no loss of pride or burdensome sense of obligation in accepting his generosity. (I should add that this was related to me beforehand by Mr. Darcy as an illustration of his friend's excellent character. Sir Richard himself did not mention the matter at all, apart from his hope that I would allow him to introduce his Cousin and her daughters to my acquaintance; in deference to me and in compliance with Mr. Darcy's wishes he had not wanted to make this first party *too* large.) Sir Richard's pleasure in meeting me was certainly genuine, but the arrival of anyone new to him is probably a matter of joy and he clearly delights in collecting people about him.

Lady Mansfield cannot be more than six or seven and twenty; her face is handsome, her figure tall and striking, and her address graceful. Her manners have more elegance than her Husband's perhaps, but they would be improved by some share of his frankness and warmth. Though perfectly well-bred, she is reserved and cold, with nothing to say for herself unless it is about her several children whom we were obliged to meet and admire, and who would benefit from less indulgence by their Mother than they are in the habit of receiving. And I am sorry to say that she strikes me as the sort of woman who is determined never to be well, and who likes her spasms and nervousness and the consequence they give her, better than anything else.

Also in attendance was a Lady Ashton Dennis, a person in whom I had the greatest interest since she is reputed to place a high value on rank and consequence and in those terms would doubtless already have a decided opinion on the worth of the new Mrs. Darcy. A widow of a certain age (comfortably situated and well provided with a handsome jointure, I understand) who had been a close friend of Lady Anne Darcy, I was pleasantly surprised to find her a rational, well-mannered woman of sense with a cultivated mind; a little cool to be sure, but I believe I detected a willingness to defer judgment until she knows me better. If true, then I shall admire her integrity and delicate sense of honour.

Lady Ashton Dennis is a particular intimate of the Steventon family of Oakley Hall, who were not of the party since the head of the family, Sir James, and his daughter do not return from Bath for another two weeks. She gave me to understand, however, that he is anxious to wait upon me.

The last members of our party were Mr. Daley and his wife of less than a year, Margaret. He farms a great estate in the next parish, is perhaps seven or eight-and-thirty and a sensible, straight-forward, open-hearted man indeed. His wife, considerably his junior, is a quick-witted, clever person with an unaffected, cheerful disposition, and as fond of her Husband as he clearly is of her. As proof of his affection for his wife, he was willing to sacrifice a great deal of independence by moving from his seat at Weldon Abbey to her Father's house after their marriage. Mrs. Daley's affection and regard for her Father made it impossible for her to leave him; and his nervous disposition and hatred of change of any kind made it impossible for him to move with them to Weldon. The Daleys are well-matched, make a very fine couple, are evidently happy in each other's company, and I like them very much indeed. Mr. Daley is no false flatterer and when he remarked to me privately that he had never seen Mr. Darcy so well content and how he sincerely rejoiced in our happiness, I felt the full value of his sentiments.

On the way home Mr. Darcy was so well pleased with the occasion to remark that we should consider a ball at Pemberley this summer to coincide with Georgiana's coming out this season. This was not the first time the subject of Georgiana's coming out has been raised, but until now, afraid of displeasing her Brother I suppose, she has chosen not to discuss it, preferring rather to throw a mist over such a gloomy prospect, hoping that when the mist cleared away, she should see something else. But here it was again and she could contain herself no longer, becoming very agitated and begging her Brother to reconsider her coming out — she is but seventeen and next year would do as well — indeed would be better altogether — and she would need every minute of time between now and then to prepare herself for something so abhorrent. She became so carried away that I just had to laugh and even her Brother, astonished as he was by her vehemence, could scarce conceal a smile, whereupon Georgiana burst into tears and the rest of the journey home was spent in comforting her. It is strange, is it not? Most girls of her age and station look to their coming out as the happiest of events, but I think I understand Georgiana's reluctance to be properly launched into society. However, before venturing another of my famous hasty opinions, later to be regretted, I shall keep my own counsel until I am sure!

Your account of the party given at Longbourn in your honour amused me greatly. Mamma's excessive fawning over Mr. Bingley is hardly surprising, but the poor man must have been quite overcome by so much adoration from my Aunt Phillips, the Lucases, and all the others. Would that my Father had rescued him, 'tho I suspect he was taking his own wry pleasure in observing the sorry spectacle, with no desire to curtail his enjoyment. Yet I am sorry for the embarrassment you must have felt, dear Jane. Let us hope that all will be calmer once you are returned from town. You will not wish Mr. Bingley to be subjected to many more such displays of hollow flattery, I know. And he would certainly not wish it for himself. At least we may take comfort from the fact that with none of Bingley's family or friends in attendance, any embarrassment you suffered was for yourselves alone. A small comfort, but one worth having, nonetheless.

I trust that you are happily settled in London and that the many social demands of the city will nevertheless allow you a little time to write to your devoted Sister,

Elizabeth Darcy

Letter No. 4

Pemberley
Monday, 22^d March, 1813

*M*y dear Jane,
Having imagined you so caught up in London's pleasant distractions that your pen would be idle, yesterday's long letter from you was an unexpected pleasure. It seems Mr. Bingley is taking great pride, as indeed he should, in presenting his beautiful wife to London society and since it is your pleasure to please *him*, nothing can be lacking to make your stay in town anything less than delightful, which pleases *me*.

And so Miss Bingley is all that is affectionate and insincere — exactly as I supposed! My Aunt Gardiner, by the way, writes that she has never seen you in greater beauty and contentment, dearest Jane, adding that she and my Uncle have enjoyed improving their acquaintance with Mr. Bingley. They regard him highly — the more so since his devotion to their niece is everything they would wish to see.

How long do you plan to stay in town? Mr. Darcy has taken it into his head that his wife's portrait must hang next to his in the gallery at Pemberley and wishes to visit the Summer Exhibition at the Academy with a view to selecting a painter. For my part, I told him, there are already more than enough Darcys hanging in the gallery, and in any case, why go to the trouble of taking a likeness of merely *tolerable* beauty? A face once taken was taken for generations, I pointed out. Mr. Darcy, who slowly becomes used to my teasing, replied that it is *in*tolerable that my memory so perfectly recalls events it should have forgotten long ago. But it is settled: in May we shall visit the Academy and other portrait galleries, and a portrait there shall be. Mr. Darcy insists upon it. If you have already removed to Netherfield by that time, we will surely see you when we call at Longbourn on our way — and how I long to see you!

Poor Georgiana is still upset at the prospect of coming out formally this season and has engaged me in very long conversations on the subject. (I am honoured that she already regards our relationship as being such as allows her to confide her feelings on such a heart-felt matter.) She does not feel equal to such an ordeal — being presented at court — all the people looking at her —

the balls — next year she would face it with far more equanimity, she feels certain. Now that she feels so at home at Pemberley again, she does not wish to spend an entire season in London away from her dear Brother and Sister, knowing that Mr. Darcy and I do not plan to be away from Pemberley for so long. No, next year would be quite a different matter!

Her natural shyness and reserve are heightened, I feel, by the unfortunate episode with Mr. Wickham, which still affects her deeply. While it is too tender a subject to be entered on fully between us, I have told her that I completely understand her sentiments and feel certain that her Brother would not wish her to be unhappy. Although I have not yet had the courage to say so to her, I am now quite certain of her main fear: that once formally out in society, she will be in grave danger of being taken advantage of again and prey to fortune hunters.

As Miss Georgiana Darcy, however, certain things are expected, but her Brother will need little persuasion, I feel sure, to postpone his Sister's coming out for another year; there is nothing he would not do to promote her happiness. When Colonel Fitzwilliam arrives next month (Mr. Darcy's Cousin who has joint guardianship of Miss Darcy, and whom I first met at Rosings, you may remember) she will, I know, want to discuss this painful subject with him in the hope of persuading him to take her part. She is very fond of him, as we all are, and values his opinions highly.

Colonel Fitzwilliam usually visits Rosings in April but has decided to forgo that pleasure this year. The thought of having to listen to Lady Catherine's discourses on the polluted shades of Pemberley for weeks on end is more than even *his* easy temper can bear to contemplate.

Yesterday we dined with Sir James Steventon of Oakley Hall, which lies just a few miles from Pemberley. A handsome man of about fifty years, he is lately returned from Bath. When Lady Steventon died (an excellent woman by all accounts and another dear friend of Lady Anne) he was left with two daughters ages fourteen and twelve. Phoebe, the eldest, is now twenty-four, lately married and gone from home; Eleanor at twenty-two remains at home and seems a steady, quiet sort of girl, though with an air of disappointment about her — whether from a broken romance or no romance I cannot say, but I should like to know her better.

Her Father, in contrast, while a kindly man and a generous host, is inordinately pleased with himself and his situation and it is evident that he considers the blessing of beauty inferior only to the blessing of a baronetcy — this I realised when he showed me the Steventon of Oakley Hall entry in the Baronetage. My satirical eye found great amusement in the reverence he shows for himself. In short, vanity would seem to be the beginning and end of his character (I have seldom seen so many mirrors) but perhaps I surmise too much and judge too harshly on so short an acquaintance. Let us not forget how wrong first impressions can be! My Husband did say in passing that Sir James is rumoured to live beyond his means but not wishing to force Mr. Darcy to say anything which might be disloyal to his friend I did not pursue the subject. On reflection, though, his feelings of loyalty may have more to do with the memory of his Mother's close friendship with Lady Steventon.

We were a small party: Lady Ashton Dennis, with whom I had a pleasant conversation, and the young vicar of the parish of Oakley, a Mr. Randall and his wife. Mr. and Mrs. Randall make an ideal pair: he has an air of self-sufficient smugness (but without Mr. Collins's obsequiousness, I believe), while she has great pretensions to elegance. Despite these pretensions, however, Mrs. Randall is wanting in air, voice and manner, and her dress, while expensive, is overly fussy. Her mind appears totally devoid either of taste or judgement. All her ideas are towards the elegance of her appearance, the fashion of her dress and the admiration she wishes them to excite. She professes a love of books without reading, is lively without wit and generally good-humoured without merit. Of her Father, a man whose fortune was apparently earned in honest trade, we heard nothing, yet she feels all the grandeur of *her Sister* having married *very well indeed*. Her Sister, we should all know, has *two* carriages at Pine Grove and her Brother and Sister will surely bring the barouche-landau when they came to visit this summer! Such elegant stupidity!

Several times she tried to engage Mr. Darcy in conversation of this kind and I was taken aback to see that haughty, disagreeable look on his face which I had almost forgotten (though it was familiar enough at the beginning of our acquaintance, as you will also recall). Catching my eye and immediately comprehending my surprise, the expression on his dear face changed gradually from one of indignant contempt to a composed and steady gravity, very much more to my liking.

Mrs. Randall had a more willing (though not fully attentive) audience in Sir James, who, while listening to the fulsome praises of Pine Grove, (which he has doubtless heard many times before) was at the same time planning to impress in his turn with some tale or other of fashionable Bath, as soon as Mrs. Randall should draw breath. Sir James would persuade us to visit Bath — it would give me the greatest pleasure to introduce you in the very best circles — Bath is incomparable, my dear Mrs. Darcy! On finding out that I had never been there, Mrs. Randall was keen to add her own recommendation that it is advisable to mix in the world in a proper degree; Mr. Darcy ought to take his wife there without too much delay. Furthermore, it did not appear to her that life could supply any greater felicity than the pleasures of Bath.

Despite these protestations, I fear that the pleasures of Bath, fashionable and diverting as they may be, hold no attraction for me, nor I may say for Mr. Darcy and Georgiana, who having once visited there some years ago with their parents are both of the opinion that while Bath may be pleasant enough for a short visit, beyond that it is the most tiresome place in the world. If I should be in pursuit of novelty and amusement, it is to the Lakes I would wish to go. Having read Gilpin's Tour of the Lakes last year in preparation for my journey there with the Gardiners, which was then denied me, nowhere else will do! (You will recall my disappointment that my Uncle was prevented by business affairs from taking the necessary time for us to go so far. Now I am heartily grateful to him for such true devotion to commerce that we had to make do with visiting *Derbyshire* instead!) No, we are all much too comfortable in our family party at Pemberley and more than happy to be removed from society of the sort which Sir James Steventon finds superior and pleasing.

Later, I overheard Mrs. Randall remark to Lady Ashton Dennis how astonished she was to find me so lady-like! I thought it better not to mention this to Mr. Darcy, who would have been unable to share my amusement, I fear. Lady Ashton Dennis had her back to me so I was unable to overhear her reply, but as she left Mrs. Randall's side almost immediately, surmise that she had no wish to continue that particular line of conversation.

You will hardly be surprised that we were very pleased to return home to Pemberley to breathe the air of better company. Sir James, for all his vanity, is a courteous, kindly man who means well, but I dislike the Randalls and can do very well without Mrs. Randall's pert pretensions and under-bred finery. For his part, Mr. Darcy made it quite clear that he has no desire to improve *that* acquaintance so the likelihood of being often in the Randalls' company is thankfully small!

And now, dear Jane, this mild Spring day beckons me outdoors. Last night the rain beat in torrents against the windows and kept me awake a little. But we have a charming morning after it and storms and sleeplessness are nothing when they are over. I have a great desire to pick primroses, bury my nose in their damp petals, close my eyes and taking a deep breath, transport myself in an instant back to Longbourn and memories of gathering primroses with you and my Sisters on just such a day as this. On my walks I usually find enough flowers to fill a small vase for Mr. Darcy's desk. How the weeks fly by: my first offering after our arrival here was a modest bunch of snowdrops; since then there have been sweet violets and early wild daffodils. Mr. Darcy has never asked whence the flowers come and I have never mentioned it, but perhaps he has some notion of their being a small token of his wife's deep regard and affection.

Tomorrow, Georgiana accompanies me to visit the poor. Let us hope for another fine day such as this one for our excursion. Our needles have been flying during the cold days of winter, for together we have made a handsome basketful of shifts, caps, blankets and baby linen to distribute. Mr. Darcy, I am proud to say, shows a keen interest in these calls and is always grateful to know of a situation where he might be materially helpful. (You may recall that even Mr. Wickham owned that Mr. Darcy was liberal and generous in assisting his tenants and relieving the poor, though he mistakenly chose to believe he was motivated solely by family and filial pride.)

Yes, I also received a letter from Lydia that they are moving quarters and in need of help to settle their bills. While this is hardly a subject I would wish to discuss with Mr. Darcy, I shall send what I can privately, though not with any false hope that by so doing they might resolve to live within their means in future.

I am most interested in what you say about the latest styles in London though I am uncertain whether I shall like my petticoat showing a full foot beneath my skirt even with a prettily trimmed hem. Your new walking dress will be very smart indeed — the Turkey red gown contrasting beautifully with your fair complexion — and the military-style spencer with small standing collar is an excellent thought. How grand you will look, Jane!

In anticipation of our being in town, Georgiana and I have been spending many an hour poring over the fashions in *La Belle Assemblée*. We notice (and you now confirm) that ribbon trimmings are quite the thing and I foresee us at Grafton House buying yards and yards to bring our gowns up to date. You may be sure that Mrs. Darcy of Pemberley will not bear to be outdone by her Sister Jane, and intends to be every bit as stylish as Mrs. Bingley of Netherfield!

Affectionately,
Elizabeth

Letter No. 5

*F*or your amusement, dear Jane, a postscript to my letter of yesterday.

To entertain us last evening I read aloud some of my favourite poems by Cowper (yes, from that same well-thumbed and now-tattered volume my Father gave me — Mr. Darcy would have it re-bound or get me a new copy, but I will have none of it!) Do you remember how we loved The Retired Cat and read it over and over? And the Moral:

> *Beware of too sublime a sense*
> *Of your own worth and consequence*
> *The man who dreams himself so great,*
> *And his importance of such weight*

> *That all around in all that's done*
> *Must move and act for him alone,*
> *Will learn in school of tribulation*
> *The folly of his expectation.*

As I finished reading, Mr. Darcy, who was sitting a little apart from us and had not appeared to be paying much attention, looked up and said, 'So Mr. Cowper was acquainted with Sir James Steventon, was he?' How we all laughed! I fear that henceforth we will all think of The Retired Cat as Sir James and Sir James as The Retired Cat.

Georgiana awaits me and besides, I can recollect nothing more to add to yesterday's letter. When my letter is gone, I suppose I shall.

Affectionately,
E.D.

Letter No. 6

Pemberley
Thursday, 8th April, 1813

*S*o, my dear Jane, we shall see each other at Nether-field next month, which suits me just as well as seeing you in London and will give me the additional pleasure of seeing you mistress in your own home. I think we shall not stay in town longer than it takes Mr. Darcy to conclude his business and for us to see the exhibitions. Since you and Mr. Bingley will have already left, and any arrangements for Georgiana's coming out this season are now happily postponed for another year, London will have no further claim on our time. Mr. Darcy does not wish to be too long from Pemberley and since our first wish is to see you and Mr. Bingley again, to stay at Netherfield on our way back to Pemberley will be the very thing.

If you have been wondering why I have taken so long to write — for which I beg forgiveness — we were surprised by an unexpected visit from my Father two weeks ago! He had written of his plan to come this summer but since the spring weather has been so favourable, decided he could wait no longer to see the library at Pemberley. Kitty had begged my Father to be allowed to accompany him but he was firm that she and Mary were to remain with their Mother and keep her company. My Mother, not surprisingly, was unhappy to be left alone, especially with you and Mr. Bingley gone from Netherfield, and quite certain that her nerves would suffer greatly as a consequence of being abandoned.

Indeed, a rare letter to me from my Mother which came last week indicates that my Father made his intentions to travel alone all too clear. The letter continues that, as always, she has been abominably used by everyone, especially by her daughter Elizabeth, who must have known her Father's plans and who should have insisted that her Mother not be left behind, but no, she is now too high and mighty to give a thought to her heartbroken Mother, whose health, indifferent at best, will be in grave danger following such shameful neglect, &c., &c. You may imagine the rest. While it seemed hardly worth the trouble of taking up my pen to persuade my Mother that I had not the smallest idea of his visit until he arrived, I tried my best.

My Father was quite unmoved by the uproar his announcement provoked, telling me that over many years he has perfected the art of closing his ears to unwelcome sounds, no matter how loud they may be, and that he set forth with no sense of guilt or remorse.

Unfortunately, he also set forth with very little in the way of news from Longbourn or Meryton, so I dare say I shall have to wait for news until you return to Netherfield since Kitty is by no means a diligent correspondent. Her ill-written letters have recently consisted of her boredom at home with no Jane to visit, earnest requests for an invitation to Pemberley, and little else. (Mary, of course, considers local news no more than idle gossip and therefore beneath her notice. Her infrequent letters are filled solely with reports of her study of some serious tract or other, or a new nocturne she is mastering. We are to understand that the writing of letters takes her away from these studies and one is supposed to feel grateful when she takes the trouble to write at all!)

Papa seems pleased with Pemberley and assures me that the library does not disappoint — though he expected nothing less; it has been the work of generations. Mr. Darcy has discussed his plans for improving and enlarging the library and my Father has made several useful suggestions and recommendations. I need hardly tell you what pleasure it gives me to overhear their conversations and to observe a growing mutual respect, each becoming easier in the other's company. My Father remains with us until we journey to London next month and will accompany us as far as Longbourn.

Colonel Fitzwilliam is also of our party and a very welcome guest. I may say that in his case, my first impressions have not altered upon knowing him better, quite the opposite. He is steady, observant, candid; never run away with by spirits or by selfishness; and yet, with a sensibility to what is amiable and lovely. After a morning's sport with Mr. Darcy and sometimes my Father, he will often accompany Georgiana and me on a walk or a carriage ride in the afternoon — the countryside is so delightful now that we spend as much time outdoors as possible. (My Aunt Gardiner requires detailed reports of her beloved Derbyshire as the seasons change and no great effort is needed on my part to satisfy her — I am already as enchanted by its beauties as she has always been.) The trees, though not fully clothed, are in that delightful state, when farther beauty is known to be at hand, and when, while much is actually given to the sight, more yet remains for the imagination.

Georgiana is quite transformed. Colonel Fitzwilliam, as an old and trusted friend and Cousin, has her complete confidence; she does not stand in such awe of him as she does of her Brother and it is a joy to see her happy again. Her troubled air has quite disappeared now that the feared coming out has been delayed until next year. Colonel Fitzwilliam has shown inordinate patience in listening over and over again to Georgiana's long list of reasons to postpone the feared event. Even though he and Mr. Darcy readily agreed to the postponement, she herself appears unconvinced that her wish has been granted, seeking to make her case anew in order to hear yet again that she is no danger of her guardians having changed their minds since she last mentioned the subject less than a day earlier.

There is still to be a summer ball at Pemberley (to which you will all be invited, of course). Mr. Darcy is quite set on the idea and Mrs. Reynolds scarcely conceals her delight at the prospect of a ball at Pemberley after so many years.

Yesterday, Miss Eleanor Steventon arrived for a short stay while her Father visits his married daughter. Lady Ashton Dennis's carriage comes for her in a week and she remains at Lady A.D.'s another fortnight until her Father's return.

It gave me great pleasure that she accepted my invitation to Pemberley so readily. I invited her from my own wish of wanting to know her better and thinking she might welcome a change of surroundings and society. She is so different from her Father; unassuming and quiet, not handsome in the usual way, but it is an intelligent face with grey eyes which easily see beneath the artifice and show of daily life at Oakley Hall.

Without being disrespectful of her Father, she gave me to understand that when her Mother was alive affairs at Oakley Hall were conducted very differently. Since Lady Steventon's death Lady Ashton Dennis has tried to fill her role and has been a good friend and adviser to the family, but Miss Steventon clearly misses her Mother very much. Her Sister, Phoebe, it seems, resembles her Father in every way. Although Phoebe is now married, it has made little difference to Eleanor's life since the sisters were never close, being so completely opposite in temperament.

She remembers Lady Anne Darcy very well and has fond memories of Pemberley. Mr. Darcy and Georgiana she has, of course, known since childhood but given the differences in their ages, they were never close friends then. I think Eleanor Steventon is in great need of more varied society than she is used to at Oakley Hall and in Bath, and I hope she will wish to spend more time in our company in the future. I like her very much and should dearly love to be able to dispel the aura of sadness that surrounds her.

Our days are spent quietly but are not without interest. Miss Steventon enjoys walking with me when the weather permits; otherwise we occupy ourselves happily indoors and altogether I think she is not displeased with us. You will also wish to know that she shares our fondness for the poetry of Messrs. Crabbe and Cowper.

As always, you are right. If you and I can send Lydia a little now and then *privately* to help pay the Wickhams' bills (while those bills are still of a manageable amount) that is preferable by far to the embarrassment we would both suffer in having to involve our Husbands later on when their debts accumulate into a much larger sum — as you and I both know they will. I need hardly add that any embarrassment would be for ourselves alone; the Wickhams would feel no shame at all in applying to us for assistance — but let us spare ourselves the indignity.

Georgiana begs me to join her and Miss Steventon. I had no idea of it being so late. A thick, mizzling rain keeps us indoors today. To amuse ourselves while we work, we are to read *Camilla* again. Mr. Darcy and my Father (who asks me to send you his best Fatherly love) work together in the library.

Affectionately yours,
E. Darcy

Letter No. 7

Pemberley
Friday, 23^d April, 1813

*D*earest Sister,

 I have just returned from a delightful walk on this beautiful Spring day. Pemberley abounds in fine walks and today I noticed columbines about to bloom and hints of what is to follow: the whole of the shrubbery border will be gay with pinks and sweet williams before many more weeks have passed. The syringas, too, show signs of coming out. Indeed, to sit in the shade on a fine day and look upon such pretty sights is the most perfect refreshment, is it not? For some reason, though, the smells of Spring and the wild flowers I gathered along the way today have made me very nostalgic for Longbourn and especially for you, remembering many such walks we have made together in many Springs.

No, dear Jane, do not worry, I am not unhappy (indeed, far from it), but how I wish that you and I could enjoy the present happiness of our *new* lives without having had to change anything of our *former* happy lives! I wish you had been with me on my walk today, that we could have had our usual pleasure in our own quiet company, climbed my favourite hill to seek the exquisite enjoyment of air on its summit and to admire the incomparable *Derbyshire* vista, then turned home to *Longbourn* where Mary would be reading, Kitty and Lydia trimming a bonnet, Mamma exclaiming over a piece of gossip from Aunt Phillips and Papa hidden behind the newspaper.

Such an ungrateful creature, I hear you say. There she sits in the comfort of Pemberley with a handsome, adoring Husband and his loving Sister, complaining that she would rather be elsewhere! But you would be wrong, my dear Sister; I do not complain at all. It is just that this beautiful Spring day reminds me how much I miss my family, especially you, and my reverie conjured up an ideal world where everything that used to be still is, and where Pemberley is just a brisk walk from Netherfield and Longbourn.

Now I have scolded back my senses and hasten to assure you that I am in excellent health and good humour. My Father is in good spirits and spends his days here quietly and happily, mostly in the library as you would expect, but I did persuade him yesterday to take a short walk with me as the weather was finally sunny and warm after several cold, wet days. He *said* he had enjoyed the exercise and looked forward to exploring more of Pemberley's grounds; however, when I invited him to accompany me today, he declined politely, saying he would prefer to finish the book he was reading. He and Mr. Darcy continue to enjoy each other's company. I observe an unaffected, easy kindness of manner on both sides, denoting an older acquaintance than it really is, though perhaps my imagination supplies what my eye cannot entirely reach and what my heart desires? But I think not, for Mr. Darcy has more than enough matters of business to take him from home if he chooses, yet he seeks my Father out and Papa is by no means averse to the attention.

Last week, Sir Richard Mansfield paid us a visit to introduce his widowed Cousin and her two daughters to our acquaintance. (You will recall that Sir Richard gave them a cottage on his estate after they had been left in reduced circumstances following the death of their Husband and Father.) We had a very pleasant time, and while it is clear that they still feel the loss of their Husband and Father deeply, all three made every effort to take their share in the conversation.

Mrs. Norland is very pleasant and smiling, but her smiles are more a matter of course, understandable in the circumstances. Miss Anna Norland, the elder of the two daughters at nineteen, appears to be a kind, intelligent, unaffected individual, very solicitous of the comfort of her Mother and the honour of her family. I do not perceive wit or genius, but she has sense and some degree of taste and her manners are very engaging. Something in her manner reminds me a little of Eleanor Steventon — I am not sure quite what it is — perhaps because they have both been unfairly burdened by responsibility at an early age? Or disappointed in love? But I am becoming too fanciful.

The younger Sister, Fanny, takes after her Mother; indeed, the resemblance between them is strikingly great. Fanny is an accomplished pianist and having heard of Georgiana's fine instrument asked if she might play it. Miss Norland gently chided her Sister for her boldness but Georgiana graciously took Fanny's hand and led her to the music room where we all followed and were very well entertained by both. Fanny does not have Georgiana's shyness and is probably not as moderate in temperament, but they have a love of music and poetry in common and I hope they may become good friends. Georgiana would benefit greatly from a wider acquaintance of her own age and Miss Fanny Norland cannot be more than a year or two her senior.

Sir Richard was his usual, ebullient self so that conversation was not wanting. His unaffected sincerity in the kindness he has shown to his Cousins does him great credit, the more so since he never speaks of it. I like him more and more.

Lady Mansfield, by the way, was not of the party. Fancying that one of her children *might* have a *slight* fever, she felt obliged to stay at home. She begged forgiveness and hoped that once the perhaps-slightly-feverish child was restored to good health, Mrs. Darcy, Miss Darcy and the Norlands would visit her and the children very soon. She would keep us informed of the perhaps-slightly-feverish progress. Having conveyed his wife's apologies, Sir Richard immediately improved on her invitation. Now that the weather is getting warmer, he would form a party to eat cold ham and chicken out of doors, though on reflection, perhaps it isn't *quite* warm enough yet and perhaps we should wait a month or two. Pity. But no, never mind, he'd arrange a party *indoors* and invite all the young people in the neighbourhood so that Anna and Fanny could meet other young people of their own age — can't be sitting in that cottage all day, moping. Georgiana must come too and that Steventon girl who always looks so serious. Or is she in Bath? Yes, that's it, a jolly party for the young people, the very thing.

To his great credit, Sir R. has no more pressing solicitude than that of making his Cousins happy in their new home. Their time should pass pleasantly. He has often expressed uneasiness on that head, fearing the sameness of everyday society and employments might disappoint them.

As Sir Richard was putting the finishing touches to his party, Mr. Darcy and Colonel Fitzwilliam returned home to find a very merry gathering. We were perhaps a little *too* merry for my Father, who had already retired to the library some time before. The good Colonel has now left Pemberley but promises to return in time for the ball (to take place the evening of the July full moon, the thirteenth.) His presence is a quiet one but his good humour and uncommonly amiable mind are sorely missed.

And so, my dear Jane, I hope you are just as merry in London and not exhausted from your rounds of social engagements, shops, theatres and other entertainments. Pray conserve your strength so that you will be able to take your part with equanimity in the even more demanding social life of Hertfordshire!

In an unusually worldly (but as usual, wordy) letter, Mary writes that she longs in equal measure for your return and for the delights of Mr. Bingley's library; also that Kitty is pitiful company since her good friend, Maria Lucas, has gone with Lady Lucas to Hunsford to await Charlotte's confinement. Moreover, my Mother's nerves are in a sorry state, the result of having been abandoned not only by her Husband and her Daughter Jane, but now, too, by her friend Lady Lucas, who has had the bad manners to leave the neighbourhood just when she could be of some use. Lydia never writes, Lizzy doesn't write often enough and in general Mamma finds herself quite ill-used. Poor Mary! Well, you will be home again soon and shortly thereafter we will be re-united at Longbourn. Perhaps together we will succeed in restoring Mamma to good health.

Charlotte, meanwhile, writes that since her condition has confined her to the house Lady Catherine has called on her several times at Hunsford. I have no doubt that Mr. Collins feels the very great honour she bestows upon his wife so keenly that he is obliged to express his gratitude very often and at very great length.

Yours affectionately,
Elizabeth Darcy

Letter No. 8

Grosvenor Street
Tuesday, 25th May, 1813

*D*earest Jane,

The prospect of a long quiet morning determines me to write to you. Georgiana, who joined us last week, visits family friends and Mr. Darcy pursues matters of business in the City. Both were unwilling to leave me alone and it took all my powers of persuasion to convince them that far from being a hardship, nothing would be so good for me as a little quiet cheerfulness. Much as I am enjoying our stay here, London is such a rich, spicy mixture of delights that I find I can only savour them in small portions before becoming quite giddy.

Georgiana is far better acquainted with the shops

than I am and together we have, it seems, visited every one. We return home each day with packages which are immediately opened to admire the contents anew, giving our rooms a proper air of confusion. I had no notion there were so many things we simply *had* to have, nor so many places in which to find them. Sensing my deficiency in this area, Georgiana has quietly taken the lead with a confident air, guiding her less sophisticated, country Sister from shop to shop, leading the debate between spotted, sprigged and tamboured muslin; the mull or the jackonet, and has the satisfaction of knowing herself extremely useful. While privately I may consider that dress is a frivolous distinction and that excessive solicitude about it often destroys its own aim, yet I cannot deny Georgiana the obvious pleasure she takes in these excursions and I have thus entered wholeheartedly into the spirit of it all.

How good it is to see her so at ease and happy again! I have been wondering privately whether there might be *another*, more interesting reason for this new assurance and happiness — perhaps Sir Richard's party for the young people, which finally took place shortly after we had left Pemberley, brought forth a suitor? (In the bustle of leaving and settling ourselves in Grosvenor Street, there has not yet been an opportunity for us to talk about the party, but depend upon it, I shall use all my arts to find out the particulars!) Or perhaps she is just happy to be back in London where, after all, she did spend most of her time before her Brother's marriage.

Yesterday, having just left Harding & Howell on Pall Mall (where we had both made purchases, including some silk for me in the palest of pale yellows for a new ball gown) I noticed in the window of a nearby shop — whose name I cannot for the moment recollect — the prettiest cashmere shawl in so *exactly* your favourite shade of green that I had to have it, knowing how much you would like it and how well it will look on you. In the same shop Georgiana spotted a very smart bonnet for Kitty, and together we chose some fine lace for my Mother. (Chastise me if you will, but I could not resist the temptation to also purchase some pretty handkerchiefs for my Mother since we must assume that she has worn several quite to shreds in recent weeks.) From Lydia's list of commissions (remarkably similar in length to the one which our dear Sister sent to you) I have found several items at Grafton House which I hope will find favour. It was there, too, that I spotted the pretty muslin which must be the one you described as having purchased there and decided to have a length for myself, 'tho in a pale lavender. All in all I find myself well pleased with my commissions.

It is difficult to please Mary with finery of any sort and I feel certain that a book which Mr. Darcy came across the other day while buying books for his library will give her more pleasure than anything else London's shops have to offer. I was most touched that my dear Husband bought it with Mary in mind, having had not the slightest idea that he had ever noticed the kinds of books she reads! Rather shyly, he asked if I thought it might interest her and looked quite relieved when I replied that he had chosen well — Mary would surely be as delighted with the brotherly gesture as with the book itself. Then, taking my hand, he tenderly told me how deeply certain he was that *he* had chosen well and fervently hoped that his beloved Lizzy felt similarly. I was able to tell him from the bottom of my heart that I had chosen very well indeed and could not imagine any greater happiness.

The pale yellow silk, you should know, will be embroidered all over with white glass beads (more at the hem) and will have an ivory silk collar. We found gloves to exactly match the dress so that altogether I think I shall not disgrace you when one day you invite us to a ball at Netherfield (which I already know I shall enjoy far more than the first and last ball I attended there!)

We have dined with several of Mr. Darcy's acquaintance, several of whom are exceedingly puzzled at his spending so much time in the country these days and so little in town, allowing Mr. Darcy the opportunity to relate his enthusiasm for the latest agricultural techniques and his plans to improve more of the farm land on the estates. At Pemberley he spends a good deal of time with his steward discussing the latest farming methods and his plans to drain more fields and plant more hedge-rows. Colonel Fitzwilliam amused us greatly by showing an unlikely interest in this endeavour after finding out that larger, well-drained fields separated by hedges make for much livelier fox hunting!

Yesterday, Mr. Darcy and I went to the Society of Painters Exhibition in Spring Gardens. It is not thought a good collection, but I was very well pleased. We have also seen the Great Exhibition at the British Academy and we hope to have time to see Sir Joshua Reynolds's paintings in Pall Mall. Mr. Darcy is much taken by some portraits by Mr. Henry Raeburn, a Scottish painter just elected an associate of the Royal Academy this year. An acquaintance of Mr. Darcy's tells him that Mr. Raeburn seldom travels from his studio in Edinburgh (where he sometime has four sittings in one day) and should that be so, I doubt whether the beauty of Mrs. Darcy of Pemberley will be sufficient to tempt Mr. Raeburn from Scotland! This information merely served to further spark Mr. Darcy's interest; he is not a man to be gain-said and having discovered that Mr. Raeburn is in town to receive his Academy diploma, has in mind to seek him out directly.

I know you will be interested to know that Miss Bingley and Mrs. Hurst called on Georgiana and me three days ago. I recalled (only to myself, of course) that the last time the four of us had been together was at Pemberley last summer when Miss Bingley did her very best to embarrass me in front of the Darcy family and my Uncle and Aunt Gardiner. Imagine, less than a year ago, and so many changes since that time! Their manners towards me, not surprisingly, are much improved in civility if not in sincerity, yet there is still the sameness and the elegance, the prosperity and the nothingness. Full of false sincerity, they took their leave after half an hour having made polite enquiries after dear Jane and the rest of my family. Miss Bingley could not, however, resist the opportunity to enquire after Mr. Darcy's aunt, Lady Catherine de Bourgh, and was probably disappointed by my calm, non-committal reply.

Georgiana commanded much more of their interest. They questioned her minutely on her health, her music, her accomplishments — then showered her with compliments on her good health, prodigious talents and industry. I was privately amused by one topic of their conversation: the purchase of a sprig for Mrs. Hurst's hat and whether flowers or fruit would be most becoming? Georgiana's opinion on the subject was most eagerly sought, though not your Sister's, which may surprise you. I cannot help thinking, however, that it is more natural to have flowers grow out of the head than fruit. What do you think on that subject?

Yesterday, politeness required that we return their call. When conversation turned to books, the accomplished Miss Bingley had some very disparaging remarks to make about novels and the sorts of people who read them. I felt obliged to mention that Georgiana and I are so fond of Richardson's *Sir Charles Grandison* that we plan to celebrate Sir Charles's wedding anniversary every year. Indeed, I continued, we are great novel readers and not ashamed of being so. You may imagine how quickly the tide of conversation turned to the safer shores of the weather. It is quite likely, of course, that we may cross paths with them often at evening engagements during our stay, but I feel up to their scrutiny and shall not fear them.

Dear Jane, I already hear you admonishing me for my ungenerosity towards them and my ever-satirical tongue, but I am sorry to say that I am not sorry for it. In their company I feel I will never be comfortable, nor easy, but for your sake and Mr. Bingley's I shall feign that I am.

Jane, your letter just arrived with the news that Charlotte is safely delivered of a son. What good news! I shall write to her directly. Having given birth to one sickly specimen herself, I dare say Lady Catherine de Bourgh has as much in the way of excellent advice to offer on the subject of children as on every other, but I know Charlotte will cope with her usual good sense and her child should be none the worse for the interference.

Mr. Darcy and I dine again today with my Uncle and Aunt Gardiner, giving all four of us great pleasure. Georgiana dines with a school friend. Sadly, business affairs requiring my Uncle Gardiner to be in town may prevent them from coming to Pemberley in time for the ball. We have, however, secured a promise that once the business is settled they will join us without delay. I know my Aunt longs to visit Derbyshire again and her friends in Lambton.

I confess, knowing that I shall have my dear family around me once again when you all come to Pemberley fills me with delightful anticipation. Until then, I shall content myself with the memory of our recent visit to Longbourn and Netherfield. How merry we all were and, Jane, how well and happy you looked! Mr. Bingley just as he was, only more evidently and uniformly devoted to you, and Kitty much improved. She did not once mention officers and Mr. Darcy told me with some surprise that he had actually had a sensible conversation with her on the subject of a *book* she had recently read.

Now Jane, Mamma tells me with great relish of her visits to you every day at Netherfield, often accompanied by my Aunt Phillips or Lady Lucas. Mary appears to think the library at Netherfield her own and Kitty is another daily visitor. It is insupportable that your own family's insensitive, selfish disdain of the proprieties and lack of respect for your and Mr. Bingley's privacy should put you in such an invidious position. Jane, take care that you are not overrun by relations only too anxious to share your good fortune! Your generous heart will not wish to be unkind, I know, but do not test Mr. Bingley's good nature by allowing your family free rein in your own household. It is too much to ask of him. Dear Jane, forgive my frankness, but I want nothing to cloud your and Mr. Bingley's happiness.

I will not say anything of the weather we have lately had, for if you were not aware of its being terrible here, it would be cruel to put it into your head.

Say everything kind for us to Mr. Bingley and know that I am always

Your loving and affectionate Sister,
Elizabeth

Letter No. 9

Grosvenor Street
Friday, 4th June, 1813

*M*y dear, dear Sister,

I feel quite doubtful as to when this letter will be finished for I can command very little quiet time at present, but yet I must begin, for we leave here tomorrow and it may be some little time after we return to Pemberley that I am able to write at leisure.

I must tell you without delay how relieved I am to have your letter forgiving me so generously for the impertinence of my last letter. On reflection, I realised that while my remarks may have been well-intentioned, they were impertinent nonetheless. Alas, since the letter was already sent they could not be undone. Thank you again and again for putting an early end to my suffering! You say that Mr. Bingley and yourself have spoken on the matter, and I am glad for it, but you will hear no more on the subject from *me*, I promise.

We are in the midst of leave-taking and packing. Georgiana accompanies us to Pemberley. Formerly she only spent the summer months there, but she now considers Pemberley her home and has no desire to prolong her stay in town without us, which pleases her Brother and me immensely, as you may imagine. Mr. Darcy considers this change to be a great compliment to me, entirely my doing and a measure of the deep affection Georgiana feels for me. While the compliment gives me great pleasure, I feel utterly unworthy of it. Nevertheless, I reminded him that my good qualities are entirely under his protection and he should exaggerate them as much as possible, but yes, I am delighted that my affection and regard for her are reciprocated so fully.

Mrs. Annesley, Georgiana's companion who has been visiting her Sister in the north, wrote that her Sister is unable to be left unattended and so, with many regrets, she will not be returning to us. Georgiana feels the loss of the good Mrs. Annesley, but perhaps not as much as she might have done were she not so comfortably established at Pemberley with us. Mr. Darcy has written Mrs. A. a warm letter thanking her for her loyalty and affection towards his Sister and in gratitude has settled a comfortable annuity on her — yet another example of Mr. Darcy's generous nature which still has the power to sometimes take me by surprise. (You may not know that Mrs. Annesley began her employment immediately after the unfortunate episode with Mr. Wickham when Georgiana was in very low spirits. It is almost entirely thanks to her that Georgiana has regained her bloom and recovered so well.)

No, I have been unable to discover that the famous party given by Sir Richard Mansfield was anything out of the common way. Georgiana is puzzled by my particular interest in the occasion and has little to say on the subject by way of information and nothing at all by way of satisfaction. Since there was nary a blush when I further enquired whether she had made any new acquaintance at the party, I must conclude that I was in error and that her happiness must be of a more general nature. How vexing! I was convinced she had fallen in love and was quite ready to rejoice in my cleverness at finding it out. My Husband is of the opinion that my talents must lie in quite another direction since this is not the first time I have drawn conclusions about people which later proved false. It is ungenerous of him to remind me, is it not? I detected only a smile and the smallest hint of a raised eyebrow when I declared my firm resolution to always judge and act in future with the greatest good sense, thus leaving me nothing further to do but forgive myself this defect immediately.

Mr. Darcy has lately been introduced to a Mr. Humphry Repton and is much taken with Mr. Repton's theories on what he calls 'landscape gardening'. This is a modern term which I do not pretend to fully understand, but since Mr. Repton is to come to Pemberley to discuss some plans of Mr. Darcy's to build a new servants wing, a conservatory, and to lay out some new gardens, I dare say I shall know very much more on the subject after his visit. Mr. Darcy tells me that Mr. Repton is well known and respected, and some years ago was in partnership with Mr. Nash the architect (and close friend of the Prince Regent, I understand — but I shall not hold *that* against Mr. Repton!). The library at Pemberley (so my Husband tells me) includes a copy of Mr. Repton's *Observations on the Theory and Practice of Landscape Gardening* which you may be assured I shall look into in advance of Mr. Repton's visit.

Mr. Darcy's attempts to engage Mr. Raeburn have been less successful. It is uncertain whether that gentleman is still in town. My own opinion is that upon hearing of Mr. Darcy's impossible commission, he either fled to Scotland immediately, or is in hiding until quite certain that the Darcys have quitted town. He may well feel himself unequal to the task of informing Mr. Darcy that to waste his considerable painterly skills (now acknowledged by the Academy itself!) to record merely tolerable beauty is hardly worth his own efforts or Mr. Darcy's money! Mr. Darcy says that if this is indeed so then he must write to Mr. Raeburn in Edinburgh forthwith, informing him that on the contrary, his wife's incomparable perfections are marred only by a head filled with fanciful nonsense, the result of an excellent memory and a cruel fondness for teasing an adoring Husband who surely deserves better treatment at her hand? On receipt of this letter, my Husband is certain Mr. Raeburn will wish to come to his immediate aid, hastening to Pemberley armed with paint brushes and canvas to record for posterity Mrs. Darcy's every blemish, wart and whisker in retribution for such merciless teasing! (Mr. Darcy, you see, begins to learn some of my ways and turns them to good advantage himself.)

Mr. Darcy is lately in very good spirits having discovered a new book, published only last year, with the grand and cumbersome title, *Observations on Laying Out Farms in the Scotch Style adapted to England,* written by a Mr. Loudon, who finds that the Scottish way of rotating crops produces better yields. My Husband is most anxious to discuss Mr. Loudon's experiments with his steward and also with Mr. Daley, who shares his interest in modern farming techniques. He and Mr. Darcy are often to be found engaged in long discussions where yields and drainage and cross-breeding are the unlikely subjects of very animated conversation.

So, our stay in town comes to an end and much as I have enjoyed the time spent here I shall not be too sorry to leave. We have lately been to the Lyceum Theatre and Covent Garden, where The Clandestine Marriage was the most respectable of the performances, but I wanted better acting. My Uncle and Aunt Gardiner were to have accompanied us but your favourite Cousin took a tumble that very morning while climbing a tree in the park which, even in her concern for her son, vexed my Aunt greatly as he had been forbidden to do that very thing many times before. He was carried home in great distress and, suspecting great injury, the apothecary was sent for immediately. Upon examination, a dislocated collar-bone was re-set, bruises and cuts attended to and much rest called for. My Aunt and Uncle, naturally did not feel able to leave the boy in care of the nurse in case the apothecary might be needed again, so we were obliged to forgo the great pleasure of their company that evening. Their absence probably prevented me enjoying the plays as much as I might have in happier circumstances.

Much more to my liking were my several drives around the city in an open carriage when the weather permitted. (Not that I want any such pursuit to get me out of doors, as you well know — the pleasure of walking and breathing fresh air is enough for me.) Yet I liked my solitary elegance very much and was ready to laugh all the time at my being where I was — I could not but feel that I had naturally small right to be parading about London in a Barouche!

Dear Jane, I so wish to make proper amends for my last letter (which produces most unpleasant reflections) yet sufficent explanation and apology are impossible and I cannot attempt either with satisfaction. So let me thank you again and again for your forgiveness. Would that I had some small portion of your tenderness of disposition.

Ever affectionately yours,
Elizabeth

I am delighted that the shawl pleases you and that it is indeed the exact match I hoped it would be.

Oh, let me add without delay that the little Boy is going on well. No further damage appears to have been done and the apothecary is pleased with his progress. My Aunt begs me to add that she will write to you herself once she is able to relinquish her duties in the sick-room.

Letter No. 10

*D*earest Jane,

Once again, I write to you from the comfort of my sitting room (which still does not *quite* feel mine). It was a little odd arriving back here after a full month's absence, and quite different from my arrival six months ago — not exactly coming *home*, yet there is a friendly familiarity about the place which makes me glad to be here again. Pemberley becomes less strange and the people less formidable; I begin to know their ways and to catch the best manner of conforming to them, or so I flatter myself. I know Mr. Darcy would be most upset to read my first sentences — he makes every effort to ensure my comfort and happiness, and I am deeply grateful for it, yet a little more time will be needed for me to gain that sense of *belonging* which will truly make Pemberley *home*. I wonder, perhaps, if it is even stranger for you with your former Longbourn home so close to your present Netherfield home? On the other hand, your Longbourn family spends so much time at Netherfield that... no, no, that will not do at all! I was about to make a cruel joke which would not have amused you at all, and I humbly beg forgiveness.

Mrs. Reynolds thinks and talks of little else besides the arrangements for the ball next month. We have just dispatched invitations. Poor Mrs. Reynolds, to have been deprived for so many years of the pleasure of all the work which must inevitably fall to her! I see I shall have little to do besides decide on the placement of a vase of flowers here, approve a menu there, and perhaps be allowed to decide who shall sleep in which room. Not a day goes by that Mrs. Reynolds doesn't have some new account of china that has been washed, beds aired, mahogany rubbed, linen repaired, wax candles ordered, chimneys swept — it is all quite exhausting to listen to. What a good thing we did not announce the date of the ball months ago; I fear Mrs. Reynolds would have quite worn herself out by now and would be giving orders from her sickbed. Yet I cannot deny her the obvious joy it gives her to contemplate Pemberley brimming with visitors and looking its very best, and it is a mark of her pride and loyalty that she works so hard to achieve it.

How different and how beautiful everything looks! The trees are in full leaf, flowers blooming everywhere. I long for you to be here to show you my favourite walks and views, and I am determined we shall take the carriage every day to — but no, I must be patient and not over-excite your anticipation else Pemberley will be a disappointment. I fervently hope my dear family so enjoys everything here that they will wish to come again and again. That Mr. Bingley has business in these parts is an additional joy — would that his business takes many weeks to conclude that we may prolong the pleasure of being together!

Tomorrow, Georgiana and I go to pick strawberries at Weldon Abbey, famous for its strawberry beds I am told. It promises to be another fine day, but much as I look forward to seeing the Daleys and to eating their fine berries, their company comes at a dear price: the Randalls are to be of the party. As Mr. Repton arrives today, my dear Husband will be prevented from joining us, although there is some consolation in being spared the frilly attentions of Mrs. Randall.

Yes, I have also had word from our Sister, Lydia; all too many words, as it happens. In her usual selfish manner she refuses to see the impropriety of her Husband being received at Pemberley and thinks only of the enjoyment she herself must forgo. Her last letter was filled with renewed entreaties that Mr. Darcy should be forgiving of the past now that he and Mr. Wickham are brothers, that I should not wish to deny her the pleasure of seeing her family, that she would enjoy a ball at Pemberley more than anything, especially in her new gown which, she assures me, has been much admired. Lydia is beyond the reach of any rational explanation I might attempt to make; perhaps you will have more success. In a postscript to her letter she remembered to thank me for the package sent from Grafton House, but wished the ribbons had been a darker shade of blue! Lest I forget, she also reminds me of her birthday this month and mentions several items she would not be displeased to receive to mark the occasion.

You will also have heard that it is now quite certain that my Uncle and Aunt Gardiner will be unable to leave town until late August. We have settled it that Kitty will remain at Pemberley for the duration of the Gardiners' stay; they will deliver her to Longbourn on their way home. (One wonders what Kitty will find to write about now that she is to come here! I trust that her delicate frame of mind which ill bears the least exertion, will not be overly taxed in finding a suitable subject.)

Yours very affectionately,
E. Darcy

Letter No. 11

Pemberley,
Saturday, 19th June, 1813

*M*y dear Sister,
Counting the hours as they pass until your arrival is a hopeless business since it serves only to lengthen them, yet I can scarce contain my joy that in little more than a week you will be here! Knowing you share the anticipation only adds to my own pleasure.

Meanwhile the days pass pleasantly enough, but with not much to tell of them. This morning, though, began delightfully when I found a single, perfect rose on my writing desk accompanied by a note inscribed in a familiar hand, For the Rose of My Heart. Mr. Darcy still has the power to astonish me with the strength of his affection, and when I remind myself (as I often do) how my own prejudices almost denied me this present happiness, I blush at my foolishness. Had I better sense I should be less willing to recall to your memory scenes which (since they reflect disgrace rather than credit on me) had better be forgot than remembered, but I leave you to settle the matter with yourself.

We were fortunate to have a sunny day for our outing to Weldon and even more fortunate that Mrs. Randall was indisposed and unable to join us. Mr. Randall endeavoured to make up for her absence, with little success — his manners are gentleman-like, but by no means winning. Like Sir William Lucas (but lacking that gentleman's charm) I am certain Mr. R. spends his days in a kind of slow bustle; always busy without getting on; always behindhand and lamenting it, without altering his ways.

After wandering in the gardens and picking strawberries for an hour or so we removed to the house for a cold repast, then went out again to see what had not yet been seen. And there is plenty to please the eye at Weldon. More than that, there is harmony and repose there, and I was glad to have an opportunity to tell Mr. Daley this.

Mrs. Daley particularly wishes me to tell you how much she looks forward to making your acquaintance; overhearing our conversation, Sir Richard Mansfield and the Misses Norland begged to add their own wishes to know my family. The Misses Norland are markedly improved in appearance and much more at ease — their new life suits them very well, they assured me, and the renewed bloom on their complexions confirms they speak the truth.

Lady Ashton Dennis joined us later and particularly sought me out for conversation — she understands we share a fondness for the poetry of Crabbe and Cowper and had I yet read Shelley's Queen Mab, just now published? She herself has not yet read it but heard it dismissed as "politics disguised as poetry" and was eager for my opinion. Sadly, I had none to offer, not having read it, so we had a pleasant discourse on Mr. Wordsworth's Tintern Abbey instead, then discovered a mutual enjoyment in Mary Russell Mitford's Narrative Poems on the Female Character and Our Village sketches in *Lady's Magazine*. It was pleasing (if a little surprising) to find out that she did not consider it beneath her to read *Lady's Magazine* — she may put a high value on rank and consequence, yet she is not altogether a snob and I like her all the more for it.

It was also something of an outing for the Daleys since you will recall that they live with her Father, not at the Abbey. Mr. Daley must of necessity spend a great deal of his time at Weldon running the business of his estates and, not wanting to cause hardship to loyal servants, the house is kept staffed as before. But surely he must miss living there quite dreadfully? Mr. Darcy says his friend has never mentioned that he does, but he is not the sort of person who would complain about his situation, even to so close a friend as Mr. Darcy. His devotion to his wife clearly knows no bounds and I admire him for it. He is an exceptional man.

We were glad to see Eleanor Steventon again. She is becoming a great friend of Mrs. Daley, which must be to her advantage, and Mrs. Daley's livelier temper will surely have some good effect on Eleanor's quieter disposition.

And so home to Mr. Darcy and Mr. Repton, who had spent the entire day together inspecting and discussing the house, the gardens and grounds and the best way to go about modernising and improving Pemberley. Fine as it is, nothing much has been done to it for more than a generation. Mr. Repton's notion (as I understand it) is to merge a house with its surrounding gardens, with all the main rooms at ground level and low-silled windows or French windows opening out into the garden or lawn. So, as rooms flow outside, the outside flows in, in the form of a conservatory or two attached to the house. And there you have it! The only problem is that to fully accomplish such a pretty picture at Pemberley, the servants must be moved to a new wing to be built at one side of the house (making the house look lopsided — but asymmetry is very modern and much to be desired, I am told!)

Outside they talk of enlarging the forcing gardens, improving the kitchen garden and laying out a new shrubbery. I listened to them for some time with an attention which brought me little profit, for they talked in phrases which conveyed scarcely any idea to me — my own fault entirely, having shamefully neglected Mr. Repton's work lately in favour of one of Mrs. Smith's novels. In the end I confessed to feeling so bewildered that I begged to be excused. As I told Mr. Darcy later, I am quite willing to continue my present habit of going outdoors to be outside and have no need for it to be brought indoors for my pleasure, although I do agree that the saloon, its windows opening to the ground, does admit a most refreshing view of the high wooded hills behind the house. Is it not strange, Jane, that just a few short months ago when I arrived here, the only emotions Pemberley aroused in me were intimidation and fear of inadequacy. Now I find myself rushing to its defence like a mother hen protecting her chicks! Mr. Darcy assures me that once we see the plans which Mr. Repton will draw up, it will all make perfect sense, but I am loath to see Pemberley re-modelled (especially having spent some considerable time becoming familiar with the present layout and its intricate and different ways!)

On seeing Pemberley for the first time, I remember thinking that I had never seen a place for which nature had done more, or where natural beauty had been so little counteracted by an awkward taste. Being determined not to remain in ignorance for want of asking, I returned to the subject later that evening after we had retired.

Why must there be any change at all? Mr. Darcy explained the necessity of bringing Pemberley into the modern age — his Father having done little to the house in his day — and why he wishes to engage Mr. Repton, who of all men best understands that a house should partake of its quiet and sequestered scenery and not dominate it. I must not be alarmed by Mr. Repton's pronouncement that improvement may be as well effected by the axe as the spade! Nothing shall be spoiled, I am assured; indeed Mr. Repton sees much to preserve and admire, not least the beautiful oaks and Spanish chestnuts which are as dear to my Husband as to myself and will not be disturbed.

Mr. Darcy's enthusiasm when he speaks of Pemberley knows no bounds and he is sustained in his present purpose by a conviction of its justice. Pemberley is not thrown away upon him. When he talks of remodelling and making new gardens, he proves and strengthens his attachment to the place by improving it. Mr. Repton stays a few days longer to observe and inspect and measure. He is a pleasant enough man, though my satirical eye finds his frequent compliments on his client's good taste and judgement just a little excessive. I only wish I could keep up with his notions of what is modern and desirable in a residence!

Charlotte writes of the pretty things you sent for her child, which I can well imagine, your needle always having been the lightest and nimblest of all of us. She says she recovers well from her confinement and that Lady Catherine is most attentive. She wishes, as I do, that she could join her favourite Bennets, Bingleys and Darcys at Pemberley next month, but it is not to be.

Your old-fashioned Sister sends you love and bids you adieu.

Elizabeth

Arrangements for the ball continue apace. If I were to go to the trouble of listing all those minute details which the good Mrs. Reynolds daily insists on plaguing me with, I should fill several more sheets of paper.

Letter No. 12

*D*ear, dear Jane,

    When the carriage arrived carrying a forlorn Mr.
Bingley, no Jane, and Mr. Bingley's news that ill health
obliges you to stay at Netherfield, my countenance, so
Mr. Darcy informs me, was no less shocked than when
he came upon me that dreadful day after I had just read
your letter about Lydia's elopement. This gives you an
idea of how deeply I was affected. It took me some time
to recover and welcome my Father and my Sisters as I
ought. (Though I should have welcomed some quiet
time alone to reflect, duty to my guests obliged me not to
dwell on my own disappointment.)

    Mr. Bingley is uneasy that he did not send an express before he left, but I have attempted to reassure him on that point — on the contrary, he spared me even more hours of disappointment to hang heavily on my spirits. He tells me you insisted that he come, knowing that he had business in the north which ought not to be delayed, and knowing, too, how very much he looked forward to being at Pemberley again. How like you to put his plans and pleasure before your own need of his comfort and presence! Only my Mother's determined resolve to stay with you allowed him to depart, though with great reluctance, he tells me. Pray tell Mamma how good she is to forgo her own enjoyment in remaining with you at Netherfield, and that I trust there will be many more balls at Pemberley for her to attend. We are filled with gratitude for her consideration of your welfare ahead of her own amusement.

Mr. Bingley has given me the letter you sent in his care, but I shall have to delay the pleasure of reading it until I can find a solitary moment to enjoy it fully. I need not say we are particularly anxious for your next letter to know how you get on. I send this express that you know Mr. Bingley is arrived safely.

Your loving, disappointed Sister,
Elizabeth

Letter No. 13

*M*y dear Jane,

I am all astonishment and can scarcely write! Having just read your letter to find out that I am to be an Aunt fills me with indescribable joy. I wish you every imaginable happiness which I know the event must bring. I rushed to find Mr. Bingley to offer my congratulations and found him deep in conversation with Mr. Darcy in his study. Poor Mr. Bingley! He told me of your insistence that no one but yourself should tell me the good news, and his fear that Kitty or Mary or my Father, or even he himself might inadvertently say something in an unguarded moment before I had read your letter. Now that the secret is out, we can all rejoice freely. How long have you known? How did you break the news to Mr. Bingley — pray do not spare me the particulars!

Mr. Bingley also told me — and this was the subject of his earnest discussion with Mr. Darcy which I had interrupted — that the business which brought him here (and which you had also insisted should not be postponed on your account) was nothing less than to look for an estate in Derbyshire or a neighbouring county! I stood open-mouthed for some moments trying to take in this wonderful, wonderful news, Mr. Darcy tells me, looking first at Mr. Bingley, then at him as if begging for help in comprehending it all, then back at Mr. Bingley. My dear Husband could not resist pointing out that this was the very first occasion since the beginning of our acquaintance that he had seen me rendered quite speechless. Indeed, there were so many things I wished to say that I was unequal to saying any of them. My thoughts were so bewildered, I could think of no words to suit my feeling, so instead I gave Mr. Bingley a brotherly embrace which I hope conveyed my joy more than mere words could hope to do.

Have no fear, Jane, your secret is safe with us. We realise that for many reasons it would be impolitic to announce your intentions publicly until your plans are in place and your move imminent. (Imagine Mamma's valiant attempt at secrecy — talking of it everywhere as a matter not to be talked of at present! Forgive me, I should not sport with you. Our Mother will feel your absence most keenly and you are quite right to spare her nerves for as long as possible until the event is quite certain.) Thank you for affording Mr. Darcy and me the joy of anticipating an event which will be a source of such great happiness for us all. Mr. Darcy is not unaware of how very much I miss you, though we have never spoken of it directly, and seeing how happy your news makes me adds to his own delight at the prospect of having his dearest friend established close by.

My Father and Sisters are quite settled. Kitty informed me at breakfast she was come to Pemberley to be happy and felt happy already. She and Mary are just gone into Lambton with Georgiana. My Father is with the gentlemen and Colonel Fitzwilliam, who arrived three days ago. For myself, I am slowly beginning to recover from far too much excitement (all thanks to you, dear Sister). I await Mrs. Reynolds and the cook to go over arrangements and menus once more, following which I shall go on a long walk to reflect in solitude and read your dear letter once again, to reassure myself that my most cherished wish will really be coming true and is no longer just a fanciful dream. Dear Jane, how fortunate we are that things are turning out even more happily for us than we could ever have dared to hope! I cannot help but be convinced of being favoured beyond every other human creature, in friends, fortune, circumstance and chance.

After the ball I shall write with all the particulars,

as you ask, but now duty beckons and obliges me to en-quire of Mrs. Reynolds and the cook that the musicians will arrive from London in good time, likewise the hair dresser; that enough tables are set for cards; that the supper room will be large enough and warm enough; and probably a dozen other things. Thus, by enquiring minutely into all these matters I shall have done my duty and given them the pleasure and satisfaction of being able to tell me that everything is in hand and that noth-ing will be found wanting.

Adieu. Please convey my love to my Mother. You cannot write too soon that you are feeling well again.

Ever yours,
E.D.

I have been trying on 'Aunt Elizabeth' for size. There is a certain grandeur and maturity about it which I think I shall like very well, 'tho Mr. Darcy insists that if such a title makes me *too* serious, I shall be re-named 'Aunt Lizzy' immediately. We are in agreement that the for-mality of 'Aunt Darcy' will not do at all, at least until I am *very* much older.

Letter No. 14

Pemberley,
Thursday, 15th July, 1813

$\mathcal{D}$earest Sister,
Your letter informing us of your improving health cheered us all enormously and arrived in time that we were able to enjoy the ball in better spirits than we might have expected.

In turn, I hasten to report that the occasion was a great success and much enjoyed by all, or so I am told. In truth, I hardly know. I was too much concerned that all should go well, that our guests should be comfortable, that on this first grand occasion as mistress of Pemberley I should not disgrace myself, that — no, I shall trouble you no further with my needless concerns. My Husband assures me that nothing was lacking and that he was altogether very well pleased with the evening.

Kitty is better placed than I to tell you who danced with whom and how often and the prettiest gowns — I confess I scarcely noticed — and she promises to write to you this very day with all particulars. Happily, there were plenty of partners for all the ladies so you may expect a long letter. Kitty, by the by, I find much improved in looks and manner, credit for which must be in large part due to your good influence. Indeed, she was looked at with some admiration; in her own hearing, two gentlemen pronounced her to be a pretty girl. Such words had their due effect (Georgiana tells me) and Kitty immediately thought the evening even pleasanter than she had found it before — her humble vanity was contented. Where youth and a slight diffidence are united it requires uncommon steadiness of reason to resist the attraction of being called one of the most charming girls in the room, and of being very early engaged as a partner.

Georgiana herself was quite radiant. Sir Richard Mansfield declares he has never seen her in greater beauty and is quite convinced she must be in love (though infuriatingly unenlightening as to who the object of her affections might be). Curious though I was to press him on the subject, delicacy prevailed, but should an opportunity present itself I must ask Colonel Fitzwilliam's opinion — he enjoys Georgiana's complete confidence.

During supper Eleanor Steventon told me Oakley Hall is to be let at Michaelmas and that she and her Father are to settle at Bath. (The rumours of Sir James being distressed for money are not unfounded, it would appear, but any embarrassment he may feel on that account is well concealed beneath his ample self-importance. He engaged my Father in lengthy conversation, which I am sure will have added much to Papa's studies of human folly). Poor Eleanor! To be removed to a society which will give her so little pleasure is a sad misfortune, the more since she has become good friends with the Norland sisters and is always welcome company for the Pemberley ladies. I shall be sorry to lose her and console myself with the hope that she will return often into the neighbourhood with Lady Ashton Dennis, who is a regular visitor to Bath and will surely not need much persuasion to bring her god-daughter for regular visits.

But I have digressed. I was especially concerned that the Norland girls should have an enjoyable ball. Kitty tells me they danced every dance and were much admired, the younger particularly being singled out for praise. Mrs. Norland played cards and conversed easily with her partners, I was happy to see. Her Cousin, as you would expect, was a most genial guest; Lady Mansfield, as you might also expect, reported minutely on the health of her children to anyone misguided enough to ask after them.

Mrs. Daley's father could not be persuaded to leave the comfort of his own home despite our assurances that Pemberley is not a draughty house and that a snug sitting room with a fire would be provided for him. But no, even in mid-summer there can be a chill in the evening air which, following after a warm day, can be even more injurious to health than a chilly winter night, the sudden changes in temperature being particularly harmful. The Daleys themselves were their usual, delightful selves, but more interestingly (forgive me, I should have mentioned this earlier) Mr. Daley knows of an estate some thirty miles away which may become available for purchase at the end of this year! Later this week he accompanies Mr. Bingley and Mr. Darcy to inspect it. Dare we begin to hope?

Mr. Darcy and I danced four dances together and amused ourselves recollecting the first time we had danced together at Netherfield. He wished to know was I still at work on a character sketch of him, would he be obliged to make conversation, or was he to be permitted to enjoy the dance in complete silence? I took delight in telling him that while my sketch of his character is not quite complete, it is far enough advanced that I would gladly spare him the punishment of conversation while dancing. Besides, since I had the rest of our lives to complete it, there was no immediate urgency to the matter.

After the last guests had departed, Mr. Darcy and I

stepped outside to savour the brilliancy of an unclouded
night and the contrast of the deep shade of the woods
across the stream with the liquid silver of the water in
the light of the full moon, agreeing that our first ball at
Pemberley had been a success.

All that was missing to make the occasion and our
joy complete were you, dear Sister, and my Uncle and
Aunt Gardiner, but I must not dwell on regrets.

Your dear Bingley is well and attempts to rally his
spirits though it is clear he feels your absence keenly. I
have not time or patience to give half his messages; be
satisfied that the spirit of each and every one is unalter-
able affection.

Ever yours,
Elizabeth

I cannot recollect mentioning that I wore the white silk
with the short puff sleeves and bead cording. Mr. Darcy
has had one of his Mother's tiaras re-set very prettily for
me, so I fancy I at least *looked* the part — and we know
that a woman can never be too fine while she is all in
white, do we not? You may wonder that I did not wear the
new pale yellow about which you have heard so much. I
hardly know myself, the decision was made not an hour
before I went to dress! But finding myself in the decid-
edly unfamiliar (and yes, let me admit, slightly daunt-
ing) position of mistress of a grand ball, perhaps I sought

comfort in the familiarity of a favourite — not that the yellow is unbecoming; indeed, it is every bit as pretty as I described and I have no doubt of amazing the world in it in due course!

Letter No. 15

$\mathcal{D}$earest Jane,

I have no excuse to beg for having so long delayed thanking you for your agreeable letter and for the news that you are quite restored and feeling well again. Mr. Bingley is on his way back to Netherfield having left very early this morning, anxious to be on his way now that his business here is completed, and wanting to see for himself that his dear Jane is quite herself again. He and Mr. Darcy returned only yesterday from their visit to the estate which Mr. Daley talked about at the ball. Accompanied by Mr. D. they were gone some three days and appear well pleased with what they saw there. Mr. Darcy tells me the estate has been well run but lacks the capital to modernise and make those improvements which will be necessary to ensure a profitable undertaking. In short, he considers it to be an excellent proposition and approves wholeheartedly. I understand Mr. Bingley's enthusiasm is the equal of my dear Husband's, so let us hope there will be no obstacles to bar the way, for I am quite set on the idea that you and I will be no more than thirty miles apart in the future.

While the gentlemen were gone from home, Kitty, Mary and I paid a visit to the Norlands' cottage one morning, then all together we continued on to Hurstbourne Park where we were invited to dine. A severe headache obliged Georgiana to stay at Pemberley. We were none of us too disappointed to find that Lady Mansfield was gone for a few days to visit her Sister, taking all the children with her, being quite unable to be separated from them for even a day. Without the subduing influence of his wife, Sir Richard was even more ebullient than usual and we were a very merry party indeed.

After dinner, Kitty, Mary and Fanny entertained us with music and Anna Norland and I had the opportunity to discuss some verses by Mr. Crabbe which I had lately sent to her. Her gentleness of manner and an engaging address endear her to me more and more, and she particularly wished me to tell you how much she regrets that you were unable to be with us.

The next day we were invited to dine with Mrs. Daley and her Father, who amused us greatly by his concern for our health: Mrs. Darcy should not go outdoors into the garden without a little shawl (even though the day was one of the hottest yet this summer) — Miss Bennet's parasol is a little small; he is afraid she is not well-protected from the sun — Miss Georgiana Darcy is very pale; she ought to sit quietly indoors — we should all be careful walking on the grass for fear of getting our feet wet. Yes, yes, the sun may have dried the grass, but for the sake of our health and complexions we should stay in the shade where there may still be damp spots, even in the afternoon. Dear Margaret Daley is a paragon and bears her Father's idiosyncrasies with equanimity and infinite patience.

Another day we drove to Lambton to show Kitty and Mary where their Aunt Gardiner spent her childhood, then to some scenic spots to admire the incomparable beauty of the Peaks. I trust it will be in their power to tell you they have spent their time here not unpleasantly.

Today I feel just a little forlorn: my Father and Mary and your Mr. Bingley gone; Colonel Fitzwilliam already left us some days ago. Kitty sits here quietly at her work while I finish this letter; Georgiana plays a mournful song at her instrument. She assures me she is quite well; the headache which prevented her joining us at the Mansfields is gone but she has been very quiet since. She can neither sit still, not employ herself for ten minutes altogether. With an endeavour to do right, she applies to her work, but after a few minutes sinks again without knowing it herself, into languor and listlessness, moving herself in her chair, from the irritation of weariness, much oftener than she moves her needle. It is as incomprehensible as it is mortifying that she feels unable to share the burden of her unhappiness with me or her Brother. How we should like to give her comfort, yet until she feels able to open her heart we must feign a happy indifference, since to question her directly or otherwise show concern only serves to make her retreat further and pretend a cheerfulness which fools none of us — she has never wanted comfort more.

How pleasant that you have Charlotte for company until Mr. Bingley returns! Yes, I can well imagine Lady Lucas parading her prize grandchild around the neighbourhood (especially at Longbourn, of course!) What a blessing that you are obliging Mamma with one of her very own in February to even the score!

Yours very affectionately,
E. Darcy

Letter No. 16

Pemberley,
Tuesday, 17th August, 1813

𝒟earest Jane,
   I find a little time before breakfast for writing and
to tell you that of course I shall be delighted to look over
the Great House on your behalf if you and Mr. Bingley
wish it. Mr. Darcy agrees that a man is not half so aware
as a woman of draughty rooms and dampness and sees a
house with a very different eye. Mr. Bingley has made a
similar request of Mr. Darcy to look again at certain
business matters concerning the estate. With your permission, we have in mind that once the Gardiners are
here in ten days, we shall make an excursion there altogether, taking with us Mr. Darcy's steward — a man in
whom Mr. Darcy places complete trust, and whose supe-

rior knowledge and opinion he relies upon and values. (Although it is harvest time, Mr. Darcy feels confident that everything here is well under way and in capable hands.) We shall mention nothing to the Gardiners of this scheme until you agree to it, though I think you may rely on my Uncle and Aunt's discretion not to reveal your plans. Kitty has accepted an invitation from the Norlands to stay several days with them, so we would be spared any awkwardness in keeping your secret from her; she would know nothing of the real purpose of our journey. You may depend on us making a thorough inspection of the place and I shall take particular care to see that the nursery will be comfortable enough for my nephew or niece.

Since everyone left us Kitty and I have spent our days very pleasantly: two or three little dinner parties at home, some delightful drives in the curricle, quiet afternoons with Eleanor Steventon one day and with the Norlands another, have been the sum of our doings.

We have also been enthusiastically adding ribbon trims to our gowns. Kitty has trimmed a bonnet afresh very prettily — and we are all stitching some very *tiny* garments which we hope will please you. We would not have you think that our days are spent in complete idleness. Indeed, not an hour in the day hangs heavy on our hands. When not engaged, we read, we work, we walk, and when fatigued with these employments, relieve our spirits either by a lively song, or by some smart bon-mot and witty repartee. Although our family party is much reduced, we find ourselves so self-sufficient that it is often eleven o'clock before we quit the supper room.

No, I have had no further news from Lydia since the letter I mentioned previously, but I am not worried that something may be amiss, as her health allows her to write long letters to my Mother about ill use and neglect at the hand of her Sister, Elizabeth. It will hardly surprise you that she chose not to mention to Mamma that the very same cruel Sister Elizabeth had sent two very handsome parcels from town.

If Charlotte is still in the neighbourhood, pray send her my love. When she last wrote, her plans for returning to Hunsford were not yet fixed. She did not say as much, but we understand from Colonel Fitzwilliam that Lady Catherine has in mind to visit her Brother (the Colonel's Father) in August, so perhaps clever Charlotte wishes to delay her return until Lady C. is safely gone from Rosings Park? Pray tell her I shall write to Hunsford and to expect a letter from me there.

Yours affectionately,
Elizabeth

Letter No. 17

My dear Sister,
We are safely returned from our inspection of the Bingley estate (how well that sounds!) and I hasten to tell you that the Great House was very much admired by your Sister and your Aunt, who, you should know, is quite beside herself with joy at the prospect of having not just one, but *two* Nieces established in her favourite part of the country both of whom, she dares to hope, will invite her *very* often for *very* long, leisurely visits in the future! Nonetheless, we were scrupulous not to let our desire to have you so close to Pemberley prejudice our opinion, and were quite determined to do our best to see everything through your eyes in a proper, dispassionate

manner. In truth, my Aunt was probably the more impartial observer, but since she and I were in agreement on our observations, you may be sure that our findings are sensible and not coloured by selfish enthusiasms.

We did not count and measure rooms and windows — Mr. Bingley will surely have provided all those particulars — but rather took notice of *views* from windows and the *comfort* of rooms. The Great House is reached by means of a smooth level road of fine gravel and stands low in a valley, sheltered from the north and east by rising woods of ancient oaks. It is an imposing building and in style is not dissimilar to Netherfield, but with walls of grey stone. The grounds are a little formal perhaps, but you will recall that I was recently much in the company of Mr. Repton whose philosophies have no doubt insinuated themselves into my head, which in any case inclines more to a natural informality, as you well know. Yet the gardens are not unattractive in their formality and are laid out without awkwardness of taste. I should especially love to see the Snowdrop Grove in bloom next year — imagine, two acres of nodding white heads drifting down to a circular pond, what a harbinger of Spring!

We all agreed that the shrubbery is very fine indeed, a little larger perhaps than that at Longbourn and of equal merit. It is a rustic shrubbery with occasional seats and is called 'The Wood Walk', according to the gardener. In case Mr. Bingley did not mention it, there is a considerable and very pretty diamond-shaped walled kitchen garden with espaliered apple and pear trees numbering more than one hundred and twenty, and strawberry beds to rival those at Weldon — Mr. Daley himself said as much! Depend upon it, we shall invite ourselves next year when the berries are well ripened! We were informed by the head gardener that the present owner's Father, who had laid out the garden, was fond of good fruit, hence the number of hot-houses to be seen. We are to understand that the quantities of small fruits produced here exceed anything you can form an idea of — and remembering your fondness for pineapples, you will also wish to know that the hothouses include a pinery, 'tho it had yielded only one hundred last year!

My Aunt and I were equally delighted with the interior of the house. Rooms are well-proportioned, light and airy. For the most part large windows look out onto very pleasing prospects (the view from the drawing room being particularly attractive, facing a pretty lake with some fine chestnut trees on its banks leading to gently sloping, wooded hills in the background.) As at Pemberley, the saloon (a noble room) has a northern aspect, delightful in summer. The housekeeper — a sensible, intelligent woman — gave us to understand that the house is by no means draughty; on the contrary, in winter the rooms are snug with good fireplaces throughout. As for the private apartments, you will find the walls tastefully papered, the floors carpeted and the windows neither less perfect nor more dim than those of the drawing room below; the furniture, though not of the latest fashion, is handsome and comfortable. In short, they were warmly admired by your Aunt and Sister, who had great fun choosing where they shall stay in *your* house. As for your own apartment, you will find it well-proportioned, with a handsome bed, a bright Bath stove, mahogany wardrobes and two comfortable chairs on which the beams of a western sun pour through two sash windows.

Yes, we are of Mr. Bingley's opinion: in general, the panelling and plasterwork decoration are a little old-fashioned to be sure, but not over-bearing and add to the general feeling of comfort about the place. Several rooms put us in mind of Netherfield, which is hardly to be wondered at, both houses being of a similar period. Have I mentioned the two fine shining oak staircases and long wide gallery? The beauty of its wood and ornaments of rich carving ought to be pointed out. Aunt Gardiner, with more experience in such matters than I, declared the nursery to be everything it ought to be and satisfactory in every way.

The kitchen and domestic offices are surprisingly modern and well-equipped. No shapeless pantries and comfortless sculleries here; on the contrary they are commodious and roomy. Should you wish it, the house-keeper offers to send you particulars on servants' quarters and such.

Have I forgotten anything? My Aunt Gardiner has
obliged me by reading the foregoing and begs me to add
only that she concludes you would be every bit as happy
in the Great House as she will be to come for very long
visits. For his part, Mr. Darcy tells me he sees nothing to
prevent the purchase being speedily concluded, his
steward having satisfied him on several points about
which he will be writing to Mr. Bingley directly.

I am now quite determined to think no more about
the matter until I hear from you that all is settled. If I am
to suffer disappointment, it will be all the greater if I
have allowed myself the luxury of fanning the flames of
an already burning anticipation.

Our journey homeward took us through some very
pretty villages, in one of which resided a former
schoolfellow and intimate of my Aunt's, a Mrs. Harville,
whom she had seen only once since their respective
marriages, and that many years ago. Compliments on
good looks passed; and, after observing how time had
slipped away since they were last together, and what a
pleasure it was to see an old friend, they proceeded to
make enquiries and give intelligence as to their Fami-
lies, Sisters and Cousins. As it was such a pleasant day
and the countryside thereabouts being quite delightful,
Mr. Darcy suggested that we three take a leisurely walk,
allowing the two ladies the pleasure of enjoying their
reminiscences unencumbered. His kind suggestion was

very well received and much appreciated. Returning from our walk we were kindly invited by Mrs. Harville to take refreshment before resuming our journey homeward. Mr. Harville is presently away on business but his wife hopes there will be many occasions in the future for my Aunt and her family to make his acquaintance. So you see, Jane, the happiness of many depends on the Bingleys setting up home hereabouts! But no, I said I would say no more about it and here I am, in danger of becoming every bit as silly as our Sister, Lydia — forgive me!

I mentioned that the Norlands had invited Kitty to spend a few days with them, and arranging her visit to fit our own plans was easily accomplished. Kitty is eager to become better acquainted with the family, and Sir Richard had hinted at arranging another small party for them all — how obliging he is! Georgiana had already planned a last visit to Eleanor Steventon before her removal to Bath next month, and stays with her at Oakley Hall a week at least. I hope we will find Georgiana in better spirits when she returns. She does her best to persuade us that nothing is amiss but I am not deceived. To be sure, there will be an air of melancholy at Oakley, but Georgiana will wish to cheer her friend Eleanor and in so doing perhaps she will succeed in cheering herself. Friendship is certainly the finest balm. My Aunt's opinion is that Georgiana is quite aware that she is surrounded by a loving family with only her best interest at heart and no greater wish than her own happiness. If there are matters which she feels only she can resolve then we must be patient and respect her privacy.

And now my Aunt awaits me. It is another warm, sunny day and nothing but a ride around the park will give her pleasure. I would much rather be on foot, but my Aunt is not a great walker and has requested her favourite low phaeton with a nice little pair of ponies. I am happy to oblige her. On our return we shall likely lounge away our time with sofas, chit-chat and Quarterly Reviews till the return of the others — Mr. Gardiner from an afternoon's fishing; Mr. Darcy from business with his steward — and the arrival of dinner, during which (as you would expect) the wit and charms of your Aunt and Sister will doubtless shine resplendent in the conversation and enchant them all. You find us very happy and content with our leisurely day. My Aunt asks me to send her love to you.

> Affectionately,
> Elizabeth Darcy

Does my Father join Mr. Bingley to shoot partridge on the 1st, or does my Mother insist that Mr. Bingley come to Longbourn?

Letter No. 18

𝓜y dear Jane,

Today finds your Sister feeling quite abandoned and melancholy and uncommonly out of spirits. This dull, rainy day is most unhelpful when a long, brisk walk would be just the thing to restore my good humour. At church this morning our family pew was quite empty having been kept well-stocked these past couple of months. The Gardiners and Kitty must be close to Long-bourn by now and it will be your turn to enjoy the great pleasure of their company, though I fear it will not be for long: my Aunt is eager to be reunited with her children and my Uncle anxious to attend to his business after a long absence.

No, I do not recollect the number of chandeliers in the public rooms, but the drawing room and dining room in particular are of such a good size that surely there must be at least two in each? Likewise the saloon with its northern aspect. We were there by day, of course, and a bright, sunny day at that, so I did not think to look — forgive me. The housekeeper will be able to furnish this information, I am sure, and my Aunt may remember, so do ask her.

I think you will find our Sister, Kitty, even more improved in look and manner. She is become an excellent companion and I shall welcome another visit from her. She tells me that both Eleanor Steventon and Fanny Norland have asked her to write to them (the embraces and promises of the parting friends may be fancied), and I shall encourage my Father to allow her to visit Bath if Eleanor is kind enough to invite her there. Eleanor is a steadying influence and would be a good companion for Kitty — and in her new situation dear Eleanor will be in even *greater* need of the pleasant, intelligent conversation that our Sister is now able to provide.

Last Thursday we had a pleasant party to bid our guests farewell. The Daleys, Mansfields, Norlands, Steventons and Lady Ashton Dennis were all in attendance — the last time we shall all be together for some little while, I fear, so the occasion was one for smiles rather than laughter. Lady Ashton Dennis leaves for Bath tomorrow, the Steventons follow before Michaelmas. Oh dear, I am in danger of becoming melancholy and must say no more — so to amuse you, let me just add that Kitty shed a tear or two after the party as she told me how very much she will miss Pemberley and her new friends. I told her how delighted I am that her stay with us has not been unpleasant, yet could not resist reminding her that barely a year ago her tears were reserved exclusively for officers about to quit Meryton, and a Sister about to follow them to Brighton, whereupon we both marvelled at the changes this year has brought us, changes we could hardly have imagined at that time.

Forgive me, dear Jane, it is unfair to you that my pen refuses to write a cheerful line. I am getting too near to complaint and shall burden you no longer. Pray do not worry, I am in good health and you know that I shall laugh myself back to good sense very soon. A fine day and a long walk are all that are required.

Kitty has with her the little garments that she and I stitched for our nephew or niece. I hope you will like them.

Ever yours affectionately,
Elizabeth Darcy

Evening: I was languid and dull and very bad company when I wrote the above; I am better now. Tomorrow promises very pleasant, genial weather, which will exactly do for me — air and exercise are all I want.

Letter No. 19

*Y*our kind letter, my dearest Jane, found me in bed, for in spite of my hopes and promises when I wrote to you last, I have been indisposed. I insisted that Mr. Darcy not trouble the apothecary and indeed, I am now almost well again and recovering my strength daily.

As a consequence, I was obliged to miss Sir James Steventon's farewell party at Oakley Hall — he and Eleanor leave on Friday; the new tenants arrive immediately after Michaelmas. My intention had been to amaze the party in my new yellow gown, but it was not to be — I was destined to amaze only myself (in my nightgown) at finding myself in bed and unwell; a cruel blow to my vanity!

My dear Husband considered my indisposition an excellent reason to remain at home himself, but politeness overcame his own desires and he accompanied Georgiana to bid farewell to The Retired Cat. Most of our acquaintance were in attendance as you would expect, and by all accounts it was a merry gathering — surprisingly so given the circumstances, but Bath is now everything and the reasons for Sir James's removal there are all quite forgot. Eleanor, looking only a little pale, according to Georgiana, did her best to enter into the spirit of an occasion which must have been something of an ordeal for her: a last gathering of friends in her beloved home and the prospect of life in a city for which she has no fondness.

The dreadful Randalls, whom we successfully avoided all summer, were also there. (This news made me regret my indisposition a great deal less, I can assure you.) At first, Mr. Darcy was pleased to see Mrs. Randall intent on extolling the virtues of Bath and the wealth of her sister's Husband to Georgiana, thus being spared himself — though after more than a little time had passed, brotherly affection prompted him to extricate Georgiana from her unfortunate predicament. All manner of advice was forthcoming and freely dispensed, Georgiana tells me, from the best way to store lace to how to handle suitors (including the instruction that a woman, especially if she have the misfortune of knowing anything, should conceal it as well as she can! Moreover, it is Mrs. R.'s considered opinion that nature has given women so much in the way of understanding, that they should never find it necessary to use more than half.) In exchange for such valuable intelligence, Georgiana was expected to answer many unseemly questions about herself, her Brother and her Brother's wife. Impertinent woman! (One cannot help imagining a meeting between overbearing Mrs. Randall and imperious Lady Catherine — and both under full sail! Mr. Darcy is of the opinion that Mrs. R., easily impressed as she is by wealth, rank and finery, would be so in awe of Lady C. that she would be reduced to a simper; I am not convinced.)

The Retired Cat was in fine form, I am told. Happy to be off to enjoy the delights of Bath, he clearly looks forward to being important there. Eleanor seems resigned to her fate and Georgiana and I have attempted to cheer her by begging again and again for long visits to Pemberley as soon as she is able and as often as she wishes. I hope she is assured of the warmth and sincerity of the invitation. For my part, I shall miss the companionship of a valued friend, whose value will only increase. Georgiana shares my sentiments and together we hope to persuade dear Eleanor that we will think her very unkind if she deprives us of her company for too long.

A letter from our Sister, Lydia, arrived yesterday. Quite short, with little news other than their usual predicament of expenses outrunning income. I shall send what I can with today's post, with little expectation of thanks or repayment. Rather pointedly, she added that they had dined upon goose at Michaelmas 'to bring them good fortune and financial luck.' I shall not trouble myself to suggest that with a little restraint and prudence on their part they would not need to place quite so much reliance upon the traditional Michaelmas goose.

Did Charlotte tell you that Lady Catherine made a handsome gift of a silver cup to her son to mark his christening? Mr. Collins will surely be so overcome by her ladyship's benevolence and generosity that he will feel himself obliged to go to Rosings even more often to pay his respects and offer thanks. Never was such kindness bestowed on a more grateful object.

Affectionately,
E.D.

Letter No. 20

Pemberley,
Friday, 1st October, 1813

$\mathcal{I}$ know of no better way, my dearest Jane, of thanking you for your most affectionate concern for me than by telling you that I am quite myself again. Indeed, I am just now returned from a very long walk and feel quite envigorated by the crisp autumn air.

How pleased I am to know that arrangements for the purchase of the estate are progressing satisfactorily! Yet I shall continue to refrain from becoming over-excited for can it really be true? Every happy thought I have on the subject is immediately cancelled by another that something or other *must* prevent a satisfactory conclusion — too many people who are blessed already with abundant shares of happiness in their lives will be perhaps made far *too* happy, thus over-burdening the scales of happiness. Surely a healthy dose of disappointment is required to set the scales into a proper balance again? Dear Jane, I fear I must be a little lightheaded still — but can it really be wrong to wish for something so much?

You ask if Georgiana is in better spirits. I am happy to report that she improves daily and has more colour in her cheeks than in recent weeks. Her improvement has encouraged me to attempt to discover the reasons for her sadness but I have got nowhere. In so many ways we are very close with an ever-deepening regard for one another, but as soon as conversation threatens to turn to matters of the heart, she retreats into her shy shell as she assures me that her heart is quite free and that her affections are not engaged, but it is said in such a manner (and with that feigned lightness of heart I have seen all too often in recent weeks) as to dissuade further enquiry. No matter, I am only a little hurt that she feels unable to confide fully in me; seeing her happier and cheerful again is enough for the moment.

More cheerful news: Mr. Darcy is quite excited at Mr. Repton's preliminary plans for the new servants' wing and other improvements which I wrote you about some months ago. Delightful watercolour sketches with hinged overlays to show the results of the recommended improvements accompanied his plans, which have quite won me over, and I am now fully convinced that Mr.

Repton is a man of sensitivity and taste who does not advocate changing the *status quo* for the sake of change itself, but rather will leave that well alone for which any further 'improvement' would have exactly the opposite effect. As I made my thoughts known to Mr. Darcy, I noticed a quizzical smile, but continued on regardless in my approbation of Mr. Repton and his plans, that he should know I have entirely overcome my earlier doubts. He then began to laugh — he had not realised until that moment how very fond his dear Lizzy has become of Pemberley, else why was she previously so anxious and now so relieved? (Indeed, he must be right; I had not fully realised it myself. Since this conversation the subject has been on my mind and I think I may safely conclude that Pemberley is now my *home*, not just the grand bricks and mortar that have sheltered — and sometimes intimidated — me for almost a year, but a place in my heart which commands deep affection and respect.)

Consequently, I have informed Mr. Darcy that when Mr. Repton visits Pemberley again I should welcome his advice about some small changes to my sitting room — there!

Ever yours,
Lizzy

Letter No. 21

Pemberley,
Saturday, 16th October, 1813

$\mathcal{M}$y dear Jane,

Your most agreeable letter brought such great joy that I hasten to reply immediately. Shall you really be here by Christmas? How speedily the business has been concluded! You ask my advice on how to break this news to our Mother and I have taken the liberty of conferring with Mr. Darcy who has lately had to exercise all his powers of diplomacy concerning some feuding tenants, and therefore might have something to contribute to another, equally delicate matter.

Mr. Darcy's idea is to invite all my dear family to Pemberley for the Christmas festivities — the Gardiners, too, if they are able to come. In this manner you would *all be leaving together*. My Mother has yet to come to Pemberley and we dare to flatter ourselves that the anticipation of having her whole family together again, and seeing Pemberley and the Great House will soften the blow of you quitting Netherfield entirely. It may be impertinent of me to make the suggestion (in which case, forgive me and say no more about it) but I feel certain that were you to ask Mamma to remain with you at the Great House until your lying-in, stressing that her presence would be the greatest comfort to you, then the blow would hardly be felt at all until her eventual return to Longbourn, at which time she will be so busy regaling the neighbourhood with stories of her stay in Derbyshire and endless, minute details of her daughters' situations that she will not have a moment to regret your loss. If you and Mr. Bingley agree with this scheme, we will issue an invitation for Christmas forthwith.

Jane, much as I long to see you, forgive me if I question the wisdom of you making this journey at all not three months before your confinement? I know you are in good health and you say the physician sees no reason why you should not travel in a comfortable carriage on good roads. I suppose that should be enough to satisfy me, and reassure myself that Mr. Bingley would not allow it if he felt there was even the remotest chance of endangering your welfare. I understand your longing to see your new surroundings and your desire to have your child born at the Great House; I would want nothing less for myself, I know. You are too level-headed and sensible to put yourself in danger, and your generous, sweet nature would not wish to bring unhappiness to your loved ones, so I must trust your judgement that your decision is the right one and shall worry no more.

Colonel Fitzwilliam is expected momentarily. We all look forward to the prospect of his genial company. No doubt he will bring us news of Rosings Park, none of which will contain a single flattering word about your devoted Sister,

Elizabeth

Letter No. 22

*M*y dear Jane,

I write in desperate haste to tell you that the invitations to Longbourn and Gracechurch Street to spend Christmas at Pemberley have been dispatched, so you are free to announce your plans. I feel confident everything will work out well.

You will forgive me if I conclude abruptly, but we are all in shock at some startling news. After church yesterday, Colonel Fitzwilliam announced to Mr. Darcy that he and Georgiana had come to an understanding, that she had consented to be his wife, and he therefore begged Mr. Darcy's blessing and his permission to announce their engagement!

As soon as I am able to think clearly I shall write again. Meanwhile, I beg you not to broadcast the news, except to Mr. Bingley, of course. Be assured that we are otherwise all quite well and remain

Ever yours,
E.D.

Letter No. 23

*A*t last, dear Jane, calm has returned to Pemberley and I pick up my pen to acquaint you with
all the particulars of recent events which must have
caused you almost as much surprise as they did us. The
cold wind blows a driving rain outdoors so there will be
nothing to tempt me from my warm fire until I have quite
done and I shall attempt to leave nothing out.

After Colonel Fitzwilliam's interview with his
Cousin (of which I had no knowledge at the time) Mr.
Darcy sent word for me to join him in his study. When I
arrived and saw his face I immediately rushed to his
side in alarm. His countenance was so shocked and pale
that I thought we must be ruined or that some other grave

disaster had befallen us. So deeply shocked was he that it was hard to make any immediate sense of what he was saying. I insisted on his taking a glass of brandy to steady his nerves and in a short while he had regained his composure sufficiently to tell me all there was to know. He was then obliged to repeat every word, for what he had said seemed inconceivable, incredible, impossible!

I knew, of course, that the Colonel and Georgiana have always been fond of one another. He has, as you know, joint guardianship of her. When this mutual regard changed to a deeper affection dates from last March when Georgiana's coming out was discussed. She had sought his advice and comfort and begged him to take her part in persuading her Brother to postpone the feared event. When they both realised what was happening, Colonel Fitzwilliam made valiant efforts to persuade himself and her that such an attachment would be ill-advised (his position as her guardian and their difference in age being the prime reasons given; he also feared that she confused her affection for him with a desire for a Father figure) and he removed himself from Pemberley as soon as politeness allowed.

He returned for the ball in July to find that separation had only served to deepen their affection. Georgiana begged him to speak to her Brother there and then, Colonel Fitzwilliam demurring on the grounds that they must be absolutely sure, extracting from her a promise to think rationally and carefully on the matter until his return in October. For his part, he promised to speak to her Brother if her feelings remained unchanged — he knew that his mind was made up, but wished her to have the opportunity to change hers. He also feared jeopardising a close and valued friendship with his Cousin, Mr. Darcy, whom he did not wish to hurt or offend.

In conclusion, he declared to Mr. Darcy that while he cherishes the tenderest, deepest affection for Georgiana, if his Cousin is absolutely against their union he will abide by his wishes and make the necessary legal arrangements to remove himself as Georgiana's joint guardian.

Mr. Darcy thanked the Colonel for his frankness and hoped he would understand if he made no immediate answer. Such surprising and unexpected news deserved his best attention and he would need some little time to think about such a momentous decision. Above all, of course, he must speak to Georgiana. They agreed to speak again in three days when the Colonel returns from Weldon. Conveniently, Mr. Daley had invited Colonel Fitzwilliam and Mr. Darcy to a shooting party there, which Mr. Darcy had already been obliged to decline owing to matters of business which could not be put off.

Having unburdened his heart to me, Mr. Darcy was quite composed again and asked for my thoughts on the matter. I was not sure quite what I thought until I began to speak; here was a set of circumstances I had never imagined: two people, both now very dear to me — and by virtue of their long association, even dearer to my Husband — whom we had never contemplated in any other wise than as a cherished Sister and Cousin. It would require some effort to see them as companions for life, as husband and wife. Yet, as I spoke, it slowly came to me that the Colonel had exactly those qualities I would wish to see in a suitable Husband for Georgiana. He is a kind, good man who well understands the fragility of her nature, her shyness and the reasons behind her reserve. Most importantly, we know him as someone who can be completely trusted to bring her happiness and security. His situation in life, family, friends, and above all his character, strict principles, just notions, good habits — all that we know so well to value, all that really is of the first importance — everything of this nature pleads his cause most strongly. Indeed, his only fault seems modesty, and is it not a fine character of which modesty is the only defect?

As for age, that should be no bar to their happiness — between Mr. Darcy and me is a difference of almost eight years; what are another three or four where there is a real affection? An even greater difference in age exists between the Daleys, the happiest of couples! Additionally (and I hesitated to mention this painful subject, but felt it material) with Colonel Fitzwilliam we need have no fear that he pursues her for her fortune. As the youngest son of an Earl, marrying a woman who is well provided for is a great advantage to be sure, but we know him too well as an honest man of great integrity to enter into any doubts on *that* score. In short, his sincerity and his character do him great credit. His conduct in the present business, we must own, both towards her and towards his Cousin, has been exemplary (as he demonstrated himself in his recent interview with my Husband) and no more than I believed him perfectly equal to.

The more we spoke about it, the more convinced I became that this would not only be a suitable match, but a happy and successful one and Mr. Darcy needed little encouragement from me to agree wholeheartedly. He asked me to join him when he spoke to Georgiana. I replied that I would, gladly, but begged to have a private word with her first, that her mind should be at ease when she saw her Brother, that she should feel able to speak openly and freely, not in fear. He agreed and so I left him to his thoughts while I searched for Georgiana.

The mournful melody coming from the music room led me quickly to her. Wasting no time, I walked briskly to the piano and enquired why a woman so much in love played such a sad tune — surely something a little livelier would be more fitting? Rushing into my arms, she begged forgiveness for her strange behaviour these past months — how she hated deceiving me — her Sister, for whom she feels so much affection — such a strange time

— what will my Brother say? — tell me he has not banished the Colonel from the house — his understanding and temper answer all my wishes — dear Lizzy, so many times I have wanted to unburden myself to you! And so the tears fell and the words so long imprisoned poured forth.

It was some time before she was composed enough to hear me with equanimity, but by the time we arrived at the door to Mr. Darcy's study, arm in arm, she was a poised young woman with a tolerably stout heart able to assure her Brother rationally and sensibly (so far as any of us are truly sensible in these matters) of her attachment to Colonel Fitzwilliam and that her future happiness depended entirely on him. Her Brother, while not doubting her, wished to reassure her that she is certainly under no obligation to marry, except that which love will dictate. She then related to him at length her absolute certainty of their affections, which had stood the test of many months suspense (whether the torments of absence were softened by a clandestine correspondence, let us not enquire) and tried to explain the gradual change which her estimation of him had undergone.

Mr. Darcy declared that since this be the case, they were each deserving of the other and that he was not only willing to part with his beloved Sister, but gave her, gave them both, his heartfelt blessing. Embracing her fondly, he expressed a wish that she should have as much happiness in marriage as he has been fortunate enough to be blessed with.

So it is all settled. Have I left anything out, only to be remembered once this letter is posted? I think not, except to say that Mr. Darcy decided it would be cruel and unfair to deny Colonel Fitzwilliam another moment's happiness, and having informed his steward of the change in plan and given him instructions to handle the business which had prevented him joining the shooting party, set off for Weldon, leaving Georgiana and me the pleasure of discussing freely and at leisure a subject which for so many months has been too painful for her to speak of. Until that moment I had not realised how very much I have missed her company.

The happy pair have now left us to seek his Father's blessing, though we are to understand that that gentleman will not be surprised. Father and son are close and had already discussed the matter this summer when Colonel Fitzwilliam was at a low ebb and in need of the kind of advice he would normally have sought from Mr. Darcy.

Mr. Darcy begs me to inform you of his delight that only his second attempt at diplomacy has met with such success. (Should we really ever face total ruin, he feels certain a career in diplomacy may be his for the asking!) My Mother wrote quite effusively to thank him for the invitation; more rational thanks came from my Father and Mary; Kitty is clearly delighted to be returning so soon and looks forward to seeing her friends, especially the Norlands.

Most unfortunately, the Gardiners will not be able to join us, it being too long a journey for my Aunt at this time of year when the weather is so uncertain — but nothing will prevent their visiting their nieces (and a grand-niece or -nephew!) next summer, she promises.

Our good Mrs. Reynolds is quite beside herself with joy at the prospect of a real family Christmas again at Pemberley, regaling me with stories of past festivities which, apart from the usual charades and theatricals and Hunt the Slipper and Oranges and Lemons, culminated in a *grand ball* on Twelfth Night to which children were also invited — indeed, Mrs. Darcy, it would not be too soon to begin preparations should you wish to revive this family tradition; winter balls require copious amounts of soup and negus to greet guests on a cold night — but before Mrs. R. became too carried away with her menu I quickly changed the subject, promising to discuss the possibility with Mr. Darcy. I would not wish her to be too disappointed should Mr. Darcy decide against the scheme. Let her regrets be confined to soup and negus alone!

My dear Jane, I am exhausted, but pleasantly so, knowing that I have given you every particular on a matter which will give you reason to rejoice.

Affectionately,
Your Sister, Elizabeth

Letter No. 24

Pemberley,
Thursday, 18th November 1813

*D*earest Jane,

To own the truth, I have been laid low these past few days, merely a result of all too much excitement, the physician opines, and I am not inclined to disagree with him. Today, I feel quite restored, my recovery undoubtedly assisted by your dear letter which came yesterday, as well as another from Georgiana, who declares herself the happiest of women — the Colonel's family could not be more delighted at the match and bestowed upon her every imaginable good wish and blessing. I am so pleased for her. She and her dear Fitzwilliam will join us for Christmas but before journeying to Pemberley both feel an obligation to visit their Aunt, Lady Catherine de

Bourgh, to seek her blessing. They are at Rosings even now, and it occurs to me that perhaps this joyful event will somehow be the means of healing the breach between us. When the wedding takes place (plans for which will be discussed at our leisure after Christmas when we are all quite ourselves again) Mr. Darcy will certainly wish to invite his Aunt and surely she will not wish to snub the happy couple (or, indeed, her own Brother, Colonel Fitzwilliam's father) by not attending? Let us hope so.

A letter of an entirely different complexion from our Sister, Lydia, arrived by this morning's post. You will hardly be surprised to learn the contents in which she berates me for excluding her and her dear Wickham from the Christmas invitation — such a cruel blow — she is heartbroken and has asked Mamma to intercede on their behalf — she knows Mamma will be unable to enjoy one moment of peace until such a gross injustice is put right. I shall trouble you no further with more details as she gives me to understand that she is writing to you directly to invite herself to stay at the Great House as soon as you like. As usual, I searched the letter in vain for a word of thanks for the monetary help I lately gave to settle a bill which was about to cause deep embarrassment.

Today's post also brought a welcome letter from Eleanor Steventon announcing her return to the neighbourhood for Christmas. What a merry party we shall be! She will travel with Lady Ashton Dennis, who plans a stay of several weeks before returning to Bath. Now that her escape from Bath is imminent, she appears able to describe the tedium of her days there frankly and with a good measure of humour, but the actual experiences, I warrant, must surely require an equal measure of forbearance on her part. Knowing her love of calm and solitude, the crowded Assembly Rooms and the constant parade at the Pump Room where the ordinary course of events take place, must be insupportable. Gentlemen gather to talk over the politics of the day and compare the accounts of their newspapers; and the ladies walk about together noticing every new face and every new bonnet in the room. Not an observation is made, nor an expression used, by anyone which has not been made and used some thousands of times before under that roof, in every Bath season, she writes.

She is weary of young men whose favourite topic of conversation is themselves and who seek to impress with the intelligence that their equipage is altogether the most complete of its kind in England, their carriage the neatest, their horse the best goer, and themselves the best coachman. And equally weary of women whose idea of a spirited conversation is whether tea is as well-flavoured from the clay of Staffordshire as from that of Dresden or Sèvres. The various balls she is obliged to attend usually provoke a general dissatisfaction with everybody about her, speedily bringing on considerable weariness and a violent desire to go home!

She mentions that a fine Sunday in Bath empties every house of its inhabitants, and all the world appears on such an occasion to walk about and tell their acquaintance what a charming day it is, though there have been very few such charming days since her arrival and such dull, rainy weather as they have had can hardly have helped lift her spirits.

Dear Eleanor, how much she has to put up with, yet her sense of humour and eye for the ridiculous do not desert her. I shall write to her directly, for the knowledge that she will see Kitty again *and* have the pleasure of making your acquaintance while she is here will cheer her and add greatly to the anticipation of being among friends again.

This afternoon, the clouds which had threatened all morning cleared away bringing not only a welcome, sunny sky, but my Husband, who surprised me by offering to accompany me on a quiet walk if I felt well enough. The netting-box, just leisurely drawn forth, was closed with joyful haste, and we set out to enjoy the restorative pleasure of fresh air. Be assured, dear Jane, that I am quite well again.

Affectionately,
E.D.

Letter No. 25

Pemberley,
Wednesday, 8th December, 1813

*M*y dear, dear Jane,

This is very likely the last letter I shall write to you before you travel here. I pray that your journey will be uneventful and not too arduous, but I am so confident that Mr. Bingley will do everything in his power to prevent your becoming too tired that I am content to leave you in his capable hands and worry no further. His desire for your comfort and well-being exceeds only my own. The dry weather of this past week is a blessing and will make for pleasanter travelling and safer roads.

Yesterday was another uncommonly fine day, cold but sunny, with a sky of that intense blue one only sees on a clear winter day, and rarely in summer. When I told

Mr. Darcy, at work in his study, that I was off on a long walk, he offered to accompany me, agreeing that such a day should not be wasted indoors. Estate matters have taken much of his time lately and it had ungenerously occurred to me (but kept it to myself) that in recent weeks his steward had seen him more than his wife. (Do not admonish me, Jane, I know I am an ungrateful creature! Surely I will amend my selfish ways when I have the advantage once more of observing your tenderness of disposition at close quarters?)

Mr. Darcy was not unaware, however, and apologised for his recent neglect. Implementing more modern agricultural practices has met with some resistance among certain of the tenants who remain stubbornly convinced that the old ways are the best, and which Mr. Darcy's steward rightly felt required his intervention and tact to resolve. Then Mr. Repton's detailed plans and estimates arrived, requiring careful review and consultation with his steward and others who would be affected. By the time he had finished this explanation, we found ourselves at a favourite spot which offers a breathtaking panorama of the valley below.

I am so glad you mention Mr. Repton (said I). Next time you write to him, I beg you would mention that should he need to make alterations to the nursery wing, his work will need to be completed by June of next year at the latest.

No, no, you are quite mistaken, my dear Lizzy (said

he). No alterations are planned to that part of the house. Recollect that... and here he stopped. A long silence followed as the full import of my request permeated his understanding, followed by a flurry of activity and incomplete sentences — such joy! — quite overcome — pray, sit down — we have walked too far — can it be true? I have not seen such discomposure since Mr. Darcy's first proposal, though this time I may say his discomposure was of a more joyful nature.

Some minutes passed in this manner, then a glance between us rendered words unnecessary and we sat side by side in quiet contemplation. After a while Mr. Darcy took my hand and, pressing it to his cheek, gave me to understand that while he is not of a disposition in which happiness overflows in mirth, he wished me to know that our marriage has brought him a happiness greater than he had ever imagined to be in reserve for him. I was obliged at that moment to look away for his eyes were filled with an intensity of emotion I felt unequal to bearing. How long we sat quietly together, I cannot say; perhaps an hour or more, perhaps just a few minutes.

At last, having succeeded in convincing Mr. Darcy that yes, I was quite well enough and eager to resume our walk; that no, I would not be overtiring myself; that yes, the exercise would do me no harm at all; that no, I do not wish to be treated as an invalid, we set off again and walked several miles in a leisurely manner until we found at last, on examining our watches, that it was time to be at home.

So, dear Sister, I have obligingly furnished all the particulars to save you the trouble of enquiring — the very least I could do after my insistence on knowing how Mr. Bingley received similar news from you. Shall you like being Aunt Jane?

We had contemplated saving this news until you are all here but decided it would be churlish to deny my Mother the pleasure of informing the neighbourhood before leaving Longbourn. Poor Lady Lucas, I fear she will be outdone: she may have produced the *first* grand-child among her acquaintance, but her glory will surely be vastly diminished by my Mother's two! I must also write to Charlotte today else she will hear it first from her Mother, who has an uncanny ability to pass along gossip with lightning speed.

Dear Jane, I still expect to wake up one morning and find that this has all been a delightful dream. As I sit in the comfort of my sitting room before a good fire I look back over the past year with a sense of wonder and immense gratitude that everything has turned out so happily. Now, looking forward to a New Year I see even greater happiness and fulfillment ahead. I am not sure what I have done to deserve such blessings but I know that I cherish each and every one, every day. Perfect felicity is not the property of mortals and no one has the right to expect uninterrupted happiness. The years ahead will surely bring their share of sadness and sorrow — such is the human condition — but I know I will face whatever is to come bravely, sustained by the love and respect of my dear, kind Husband, the affections of a much loved Sister and Friend, and happy, happy memories.

Adieu, dearest Jane. I pray for your safe arrival here at Pemberley and long for the warmth of your embrace. Until we meet again, very soon, I remain,

Yours affectionately,

Lizzy

Finis

Acknowledgements

At the risk of stating the obvious, my first and greatest debt is to the genius of Jane Austen.

With the exception of a treasured hard-bound copy dated 1922 of *Love and Freindship*, a gift from a friend, Freda Fenn, my own well-worn copies of her works are humble paperbacks, but equally treasured for their enlightening introductions by Austen scholars, among them Marilyn Butler, Tony Tanner, Claude Rawson, Terry Castle, Margaret Anne Doody and of course, R.W. Chapman.

Research for this book would have taken much longer and been far less pleasurable without the Internet and the magic of the World Wide Web. Working in a rural part of New York State, where the nearest reference library of consequence is a 20-minute drive, it is hard to imagine being without them. My thanks, therefore, to those who conceived and developed the idea for what is now the Internet, including Vinton Cerf, known as the father of the Internet; and Tim Berners-Lee, who in providing the tools to create the World Wide Web in 1980, put the world at our fingertips.

Thanks also to Margaret Penston at the Royal Greenwich Observatory for information on the phases of the moon in 1813. And to Lena Young for her honest and helpful criticism.

I am also indebted to Margaret Campilonga at Chicken Soup Press for her unstinting support and unwavering enthusiasm for this book.

Finally, very special thanks to two very special people: to my patient husband, Charles Newman, for his encouragement and for understanding my need to spend so much time in the early 19th century while sometimes spending all too little in the late 20th. A computer professional, his extraordinary skills have been invaluable and more than once his expertise has prevented both my sanity and this book from being lost forever in the dark computer void. And to Jessica Newman, my stepdaughter, who, in having the courage to follow her dream, inspired me to follow mine. I wish her equal joy and fulfillment along the way.

Resources

Web sites

For anyone interested in Jane Austen in particular, or the period in general, there is an abundance of information available on-line. I hesitate to offer specific sites since this is such a fast-changing world that favourite places for research when I began this book now either no longer exist, have amalgamated with other sites, or have been replaced by even better ones. One thing is certain: search the Internet for "Jane Austen" and you will discover a treasure trove of websites covering just about everything Austen: biographies, e-texts of her works, the Jane Austen societies, the television adaptations of the books, the fashions of the period, the music, the society — it is a long list, well worth investigating.

Books

My main resources, of course, were the works and letters of Jane Austen, all of which are well-known and need not be listed here.

Less well-known, perhaps, is *Persuasions*, the journal of the Jane Austen Society of North America, published annually on December 16, Jane Austen's birthday. "Light, and bright, and sparkling" contributions to the journal are encouraged and the end result is entertaining, informative, sometimes provocative, but always worth the price of membership. Addresses for the Jane Austen societies around the world will be found on page 201.

Here is a selective list of other useful books:

Batey, Mavis. *Jane Austen and the English Landscape.* Chicago Review Press, 1996.

Beard, Geoffrey. *Craftsmen and Interior Decoration in England 1660-1820.* London: Bloomsbury, 1986.

Butler, Marilyn. *Romantics, Rebels and Reactionaries. English Literature and Its Background 1760-1830.* New York: Oxford University Press, 1981.

Birtwistle, Sue and Conklin, Susie. *The Making of Pride and Prejudice.* Penguin, 1995

————. *The Making of Emma.* Penguin, 1996.

Bush, Douglas. *Jane Austen.* New York: Macmillan, 1975

Cecil, David. *A Portrait of Jane Austen.* London: Constable, 1980

Gard, Roger. *Jane Austen's Novels: The Art of Clarity.* New Haven and London: Yale University Press, 1994.

Girouard, Mark. *Life in the English Country House.* Penguin, 1980

Honan, Park. *Jane Austen, Her Life.* New York: Fawcett Columbine, 1989.

Hubert, Maria. *Jane Austen's Christmas: The Festive Season in Georgian England.* Stroud: Sutton Publishing, 1996

Hughes, Kristine. *The Writer's Guide to Everyday Life in Regency and Victorian England, 1811-1901.* Cincinnati: Writer's Digest Books, 1998.

Lane, Maggie. *Jane Austen's World*. London: Carlton, 1997.

Nicholson, Nigel. *The World of Jane Austen*. London: Weidenfeld and Nicholson, 1991.

Pool, Daniel. *What Jane Austen Ate & Charles Dickens Knew*. New York: Simon & Schuster, 1994.

Tomalin, Claire. *Jane Austen, A Life*. New York: Alfred A. Knopf, 1997.

Tucker, George Holbert. *Jane Austen The Woman*. New York: St. Martin's Griffin, 1995.

Watkins, Susan. *Jane Austen In Style*. New York: Thames and Hudson, 1996.

Periodical

The English Garden, London, bi-monthly.

Jane Austen Societies

UNITED KINGDOM
The Jane Austen Society
Carton House
Redwood Lane
Medstead, Alton
Hampshire
GU34 5PE

UNITED STATES
The Jane Austen Society of North America
711 Cedar Lane
Villanova, PA 19085

CANADA
The Jane Austen Society of North America
22 Kingsmount Boulevard
Sudbury
Ontario
P3E 1K9

AUSTRALIA & NEW ZEALAND
The Jane Austen Society of Australia
26 Macdonald Street
Paddington
Sydney
NSW 2021
Australia

Born in Palestine, Jane Dawkins grew up in Wilton, a small country town in Wiltshire, neighbouring county to Jane Austen's Hampshire. She now resides in the rural Hudson Valley of New York State with her husband, several cats and a dog.
She has been a Jane Austen fan most of her life.

"Here's To Chicken Soup"

Chicken Soup Press

Chicken Soup Press was formed in 1995, the result of a life-long dream. Publisher, Margaret Campilonga, created the press to fulfill that dream and to honor her friend, Janet, an educator and advocate for children who died of lung cancer in 1990.

"If you have a chicken-soup friend, you have a friend for life, someone who loves you no matter what foolish things you may say or do. Janet and I used to toast to chicken soup and our friendship. The press is my way of keeping her memory alive."

We invite you to visit our website at
www.chickensouppress.com

Chicken Soup Press, Inc.
P.O. Box 164
Circleville, NY 10919
Tel.: (914) 692-6320 Fax: (914) 692-7574
Email: poet@warwick.net

If you enjoyed this book, why not give a copy to
a friend or relative as a gift?
Books can be personally autographed
(please print name)

For ordering, use the handy form below

Name:	
Address:	
City, State, Zip:	
Country:	
Phone/Fax:	
E-mail:	

Please send me .... copies of *Letters from Pemberley* at
$12 each, plus shipping and handling (US–$4, Overseas–$5
per order).
New York residents add applicable sales tax.

Total enclosed: $.............*
* We accept checks and international money orders in US dollars
only: payable to Chicken Soup Press, Inc.

Chicken Soup Press, Inc.
P.O. Box 164
Circleville, NY 10919
Tel.: (914) 692-6320/Fax: (914) 692-7574